Flip-Flop Girl

BOOKS BY KATHERINE PATERSON

KATHERINE PATERSON

Flip-Flop Girl

A TRUMPET CLUB SPECIAL EDITION

Special thanks to Virginia Fry for reading and discussing the manuscript of this book. Her comments and suggestions were invaluable to me, coming, as they do, out of her rich experiences with many children like Vinnie, Mason, and Lupe. Ms. Fry is an educator and counselor in Montpelier, Vermont, and the author of a nonfiction book of stories about creative survival among children and teenagers, to be published in 1994 by Dutton Children's Books.

Published by The Trumpet Club, Inc.,
a subsidiary of Bantam Doubleday Dell Publishing Group, Inc.,
1540 Broadway, New York, New York 10036.
"A Trumpet Club Special Edition" with the portrayal of a trumpet
and two circles is a registered trademark of
Bantam Doubleday Dell Publishing Group, Inc.

ISBN 0-440-83344-2

This edition published by arrangement with Dutton Children's
Books, a division of Penguin Books USA Inc.

Printed in the United States of America
· January 1996
1 3 5 7 9 10 8 6 4 2
OPM

Cover illustration copyright © Max Ginsburg, 1996

for
Samantha Loomis Paterson
and
Ariana Tadler Paterson
with
admiration and love

1

Mason was making monkey faces again. Jumping in front of the TV so she couldn't see the picture. Vinnie felt little bristles of anger begin to scratch away inside her chest. "Move, Mason. And stop it, right now. You can't play that silly faces game anymore. Daddy's never going to play it with you ever again."

That stopped Mason, at least for the moment. He stood staring at Vinnie with his big ghosty eyes that had dark smudges underneath. Then he made another face. This time he used the ends of his little fingers to push his nose up like a pig snout and his index fingers to pull his eyes sideways.

"I mean it, Mason. Stop it. Your face will freeze like that and then you'll be sorry." She clenched her teeth, trying to keep the anger from piercing through.

Mason added an almost toothless grin to the pig face.

"Momma!" Vinnie screamed. But it was her grandmother who stuck her head in the door. Grandma's face was round and coated with makeup. Her mouth was bright red-orange, and the lipstick bled up into the wrinkles like a little kid's painting of the sun.

"Lavinia, sweetie pie! Stop teasing your brother. C'mon now. Be a help, love. Please don't go picking on him while we're trying to pack."

She, picking on Mason? If it weren't so sad, it would be funny. Mason did nothing but torment her.

"You don't fool me, Mason," she whispered as soon as Grandma's head disappeared. "I know why you won't talk. It's just to bother me, isn't it? Well, it doesn't bother me at all, in case you're interested. I don't care if you never make another sound as long as you live. I'd like it, in fact. I can remember when you did talk. All you did was whine. Whine whine whine. I'm glad you stopped talking. Really glad."

It didn't work. Mason kept right on inventing new faces, but he never said a word.

Vinnie tried to watch the cartoon, tried to plug up the mucky feeling that leaked into her mind. She'd never told her mother about what happened the day Mason stopped talking. She had been so scared and mad. "I'm glad Daddy's dead," Mason had said. "He smelled bad."

"How dare you say that?" Vinnie had cried. "How dare you say you're glad your own daddy's dead? You're bad, bad, bad. No wonder Daddy died. Who would want to live with a kid like you?"

Mason had stared at her, wide-eyed with fright.

That evening, when they'd looked at Daddy in the coffin, Mason had tugged at Daddy's suit sleeve and said, "Get up, Daddy. Get up." She had felt a little thrill of terror. Suppose Daddy did get up out of the coffin, rise up like a vampire. What then? She had begun to shake, and

2

then she had been angry all over again. Furious, in fact, first at Daddy for being dead and then at Mason for being so stupid. "I thought you were glad, Mason. You said so your very own self. Don't say you didn't."

Mason had pretended not to hear her. "Get up." This time he'd whispered the words.

"He's dead, Mason," she'd said between her teeth so Momma couldn't hear from the other side of the room. "He's dead, and there's nothing you can say to change that."

That was the beginning of Mason's problems, the evening in the funeral home when he had looked at her with his scared, wide-eyed look. His face had been chubby then, not skinny as it was now with the blue bruises under his eyes.

But the look had frightened her all the same. "Aren't you happy, now?" she'd asked him, trying to shove away her fear. "You said yourself you were glad."

From then on, Mason had just stopped saying anything at all. Nobody but Vinnie noticed at first. They were all too upset about Daddy, but a few days later, when they saw that Mason was hardly eating as well as not talking, they slobbered all over him. They pleaded with him. They cooked his favorite foods and brought him presents. Momma would sit for hours in the big rocker, holding Mason and rocking him. Mason wasn't so dumb. He was much better off not talking than talking. He got famous for being the little boy who was so sad about his daddy's death that he could hardly eat a bite and refused to say a word.

Vinnie had lost her daddy, too. But no one seemed to care about that. No one held her and rocked her in the big chair. No one cooked spaghetti just for her or brought her presents. Daddy would have noticed. At night in bed

3

she'd pretend Daddy was still home. He was tucking her in with knock-knock jokes. "Knock knock," he'd say.

"Who's there?"

"Vinnie."

"Vinnie who?"

"Vinnie gonna give me a hug?"

And she'd laugh so much she hardly had the strength to hug him.

"Knock knock."

"Who's there?"

"Mason."

"Mason who?"

"Mason shine on you." The Mason one wasn't as good as the Vinnie one or even the Jesse one, which was the dumbest knock knock Daddy ever made up.

"Knock knock."

"Who's there?"

"Jesse."

"Jesse who?"

"Jesse minute I'm still in my underwear."

"But why is he standing outside knocking if he's in his underwear?" she'd demand.

"Knock knock."

She'd pretend to ignore him.

"Come on," he'd plead. "Just one more. This one's good."

She'd give a big, dramatic sigh. "Okay, who's there?"

"Gidget," he'd say.

"Gidget who?" she'd ask, her body already rolling up into a little knot.

"Gidget gidget gidget goo," he'd yell, tickling her until she couldn't help but giggle.

Vinnie missed him terribly, especially at bedtime. She felt so alone, even with Mason in the other bed—*especially*

4

with Mason in the other bed. She would lie awake, waiting for Daddy to come in and say good night, although she knew he wouldn't. Not ever again. He was in a grave on the other side of Washington, lying deep under the ground in a long, gray box. She wondered what it was like in the grave. What was happening to Daddy in there? Was his body all rotting and the skin falling off? She lay in her bed, trembling, her arms pressed tightly against her sides, trying not to think, listening for Daddy's step in the hall. But all she could hear was the sound of someone crying in the next room. It had to be Momma, but why would Momma be crying in the night when she never cried during the day? Why couldn't Momma come in and hold her and rock her and cry with her? Vinnie needed someone to cry with her.

But no one cared about how Vinnie was or how she felt. She had a terrible stomachache one day. She knew she was coming down with cancer. That's how Daddy got sick. He had a stomachache and it turned into cancer. She hated to tell Momma about her stomach and upset her, but she had to. If you catch cancer in time, it might not kill you. She owed it to Momma to tell her, but when Vinnie finally did tell her, Momma said she was sure it was nothing to worry about.

No matter how she felt, Vinnie was supposed to forget about herself and be the big sister and help poor little Mason. Vinnie tried to explain to her mother that Mason was playing a trick on everybody just to get attention. Her mother smiled sadly and ran her fingers through Vinnie's long hair, and the next day she took Mason to yet another doctor who she hoped would help Mason start eating right and cure him from not talking.

Her mother hardly had time to miss her daddy or do anything with Vinnie. She was always trying new things with Mason. And Mason stuck to Momma like he was some kind of second skin. Momma would have to peel him off her just to go to the bathroom. The whole time she was there, he'd stand outside the door with those big, scared eyes, as though he thought she'd disappear and never come out again.

Grandma stayed on after the funeral. She wasn't Daddy's real mother. She'd married Grandpa a couple of years before he died, when Daddy was already grown and married to Momma. You could tell she wasn't Vinnie's real grandmother because she spent all her time fussing about Mason. That meant there were two women hovering over Mason and begging him to eat just one little bite or say just one little word. It made Vinnie sick to her stomach.

She would have gone crazy if it hadn't been for Shawna Watts, who was her best friend. And now Vinnie was going to move and she wouldn't have Shawna to talk to anymore. Momma must have decided to move to Grandma's house even before Daddy died. Grandma and she had kept it a secret between the two of them. They just hadn't told Vinnie they were planning to move. Poor Daddy! They probably could hardly wait until he was dead to get out of there.

Momma thought it was wonderful to have a free house. Vinnie thought it was terrible. Who would want to live in a dumpy little town in Virginia that nobody had ever heard of?

"Of course you've heard of Brownsville," her mother said. "You've been there. That's where Grandma lives."

"Well, Shawna's never heard of it."

"Then it's up to you to tell her."

How could someone tell anyone else about a town called Brownsville? Brown was Vinnie's least favorite color. She pictured the town. Everything was brown—not even a nice brown—if any brown could be called nice, but a yellowish, grayish yucky brown. She felt sick to her stomach. Daddy would never make her move to Brownsville. He'd understand how much she'd hate it. "If I move there," she said, "it'll make me sick." I'll probably get cancer like Daddy, she thought, but she didn't say that part, because Momma never took it seriously. "I'll get really sick and it will all be because of Brownsville."

"Nonsense," her mother said without the least bit of sympathy.

Vinnie decided to work on Mason. "Tell them you'll start talking and eating right if they won't make you move."

Mason just stared at her.

"I mean it, Mason. You'll be sorry. Nobody will feel bad for you there. You won't have this great reputation for the saddest boy that ever lived. Nobody will give a doughnut hole for you. They'll probably just laugh at you and pick on you. I know about these things. I'm four years older than you."

Mason jumped up on the bed and began bouncing up and down like he was crazy.

Grandma went home for a couple of days and then came back to help them finish packing. Only you could hardly call what she did packing. It was more throwing away—throwing away everything that Vinnie needed and wanted. Grandma would have thrown Agnes away if Vinnie hadn't seen her arm poking out of a bunch of papers in the top of the trash bag. "Agnes!" Vinnie cried, snatching out her doll and scattering the papers about.

"Tell Grandma to quit throwing away all my things!" she told her mother, who was in the kitchen trying to pack dishes with Mason stuck to her shirt, Daddy's old shirt, sucking his thumb.

Her mother turned with a sigh, gently moving Mason to one side. "If you packed your own things, Vinnie—"

"I don't want to pack. I don't want to move."

"You can't have it both ways, Vinnie. If you don't want Grandma throwing away your stuff, you need to pack it yourself."

Vinnie could feel the tears starting in her eyes. She was probably going to damage her eyesight with all this crying. But this time, at least, her mother put her arm out and pulled her close. "I know it's hard for you, Vinnie. But try to understand. If we live with Grandma, we won't have to pay any rent. As hard as I work, I can't make enough to take care of us all and pay the rent, too." She kissed Vinnie's cheek.

"Suppose we move there and you can't get a job?"

"Nurses can always get jobs. They just can't get a lot of money." She pushed Vinnie's hair off her face. "Okay, sweetie?"

It was not okay, but what could Vinnie say? In spite of everything, she loved her mother. She really didn't want to make life harder for her. So Vinnie went to the tiny room that she shared with Mason and began to put her things into a plastic bag. But first she got a Magic Marker and wrote in large letters on the white plastic: "Vinnie's Things. Keep Out. Do not Touch. This means you." It made her feel a little better.

"How much further?" Vinnie knew it was a Mason kind of question, but Mason certainly wasn't going to ask anything.

Momma glanced at her in the rearview mirror, well, sort of glanced, but she was looking mostly at Mason, who was sitting up straight, staring at Momma's hair. She checked Mason out before she answered. "We haven't even gotten to Charlottesville, yet, Vinnie. Brownsville's about an hour from there, right, Mother?"

"Just about," Grandma said. "You kids need a Life Saver?"

Yes, she needed a lifesaver. One that would save her and take her back home to Washington and make her daddy alive again and let her be best friends with Shawna . . .

"Here, sweetie pie, take them." Grandma was urging the whole pack into her hand. "And share them with your brother."

Vinnie nodded.

"Thank you, Grandma," Momma prompted.

"Thank you," muttered Vinnie. The top one was red, so she popped it into her mouth, even though she knew it was Mason's favorite. She handed him a green one. "Say 'Thank you, Grandma,'" she said, knowing full well that Mason wouldn't say anything. She noticed with grim satisfaction that he put the Lifesaver in his mouth and began to suck it. He didn't have any trouble eating Lifesavers—just vegetables and meat and stuff that was good for him.

Brownsville was not all brown. It was gray. By the time they finally got there in the late afternoon, rain was coming down, soaking the boxes they carried from the U-Haul to the house. The house may have been white once, but now it looked gray. There was no grass in the tiny front yard. The little patch was brown—baked brown clay. The rain pounded against it, running off onto the gray sidewalk. Had Grandma's house always looked this dreary? She couldn't remember. The last visit they had made was before Daddy had gotten sick the first time. Mason was

9

only a baby. That time the doctors promised he would be fine. They stopped promising.

"Well," said her mother in a voice as fake and cheerful as a TV ad, "here we are."

"Welcome home," said Grandma. The little red spots of rouge made her look like a clown, Vinnie thought. Grandma unlocked the front door and rushed in ahead to turn up the thermostat. Vinnie stood in the doorway, holding one of her boxes. The house was cold and damp and dark inside. Big chairs rose in bumps like monuments in a cemetery—where Daddy lay under the ground.

Vinnie shivered. "Why are the chairs all gray?" she whispered to Momma.

Her mother tried to laugh, but that didn't help. "They're dustcovers, Vinnie. Grandma wanted to keep things nice and clean while she was gone. See—" She pulled one off a big armchair. Underneath, the chair was a fuzzy gray. "Oh," said her mother and laughed that funny laugh again.

Grandma came into the living room then and began pulling off the rest of the covers. Not all the chairs were gray, but the flowery ones seemed dingy and faded. They might as well have been gray—or brown like the huge bureaus and cupboards that loomed over the small rooms like prison guards. Vinnie was going to hate it here more than she could have imagined.

2

"Now see," her mother said, "the school is not gray."

No, it was brick—old dirty red brick with a long flight of stone steps going up to the front door. Beside the building was a concrete playground, gray like a jail yard. Here and there were cracks in the pavement, where grass and weeds had pushed their way through. Behind a high metal fence, caged like sad zoo animals collected from some other planet, were a slide, creaky-looking swings, and an ancient jungle gym.

It was still raining. It had been raining since they moved to Brownsville two days before. In her head, Vinnie had begun to call the town Graysville.

And now this dirty old school. Grandma had apologized for the way it looked. The town was planning to build a new one, she said, but times were hard and people couldn't afford more taxes.

11

"Well," said Momma, as she eyed the steep concrete stairs. "Well," she repeated, "I think the office is up yonder somewhere." She took Mason by one hand and Vinnie by the other. "Up we go." Momma had put on the cheery tone that reminded Vinnie of a TV ad. As they climbed, her mother's big shoulder bag swung and hit Vinnie in the side with every step.

Vinnie's feet hurt. Saturday Grandma had taken her to the Salvation Army and bought her three school dresses and a pair of brown leather shoes that were so new they were still stiff. Grandma was thrilled. Practically brand-new shoes at the price of secondhand ones. With her "like new" dresses and "almost new" shoes Vinnie would "look like a fourth-grade princess." Grandma crowed and chirped all the way home.

Vinnie told her mother that no one would be wearing anything but jeans and sneakers to school no matter what Grandma thought. When that didn't work, she told her mother that she would rather have her legs chopped off at the knees than wear those awful things to a new school where she didn't know anybody. Her mother laughed and then asked her please not to make Grandma unhappy. Grandma was being so kind and generous—couldn't she, just for a few days, wear the nice things that Grandma had bought for her? Later, after they saw what the other kids were wearing, then maybe— Vinnie gave up. Nobody but Daddy cared how she felt about anything. And Daddy was dead.

Vinnie let go of her mother's hand and moved slightly away. How in the world did Momma think they were going to let Mason into this stupid school anyway? Kids were supposed to talk in school, for heaven's sake. Teachers asked questions. They expected kids to answer— even if they were only in kindergarten.

But Momma marched on up the stairs to the main floor, puffing only a little as she climbed, dragging along a reluctant Mason. There was nothing for Vinnie to do but follow.

The principal was a large man, not exactly fat but big—very big. Even his voice was big. Both Mason and Vinnie backed up against Momma as he boomed down at them: "Welcome to Gertrude B. Spitzer Elementary School!"

Vinnie hated the name of the school at once. Why would a person called Gertrude have a school named after her anyway? Probably because she had been an old biddy of a principal for sixty years or something.

"Vinnie," her mother was saying, "could you sit out here with Mason while Mister—"

"*Doctor* Munchen," the principal said.

"While Doctor Munchen and I fill out the papers?" Vinnie wasn't fooled. She doubted that Mason was fooled either. This was the time for the Big Talk about Mason's Problem. Oh, dear. She sighed deeply. Gertrude B. Spitzer Elementary was going to be terrible. She just knew it. Momma pried off Mason's hand finger by finger and slipped into the office. The principal shut the door firmly behind them.

At first Mason stared at the closed door. Then he leaned his head against the panel of opaque glass, fiddling with the doorknob. "You can't go in, Mason," Vinnie whispered, feeling almost sorry for him. "Momma'll be out in a minute. Don't worry." Vinnie had hardly gotten the words out, before Mason left the door and began scurrying around the office like a demented squirrel.

The secretary barked at Vinnie. "Would you keep him under control?"

13

She jumped up to try to get Mason, but he raced away, knocking over a large trash can that clattered about, scattering stuff in every direction.

"Little girl!"

Vinnie jerked around to see a man who had come out of another office. He was short and squat, and his face was crammed together into a scowl.

Meantime, Mason had found a piece of old gum and was trying his best to chew it back to life. Vinnie grabbed him. "Mason!" She shoved her finger in his mouth to try to scoop out the gum. Mason chomped down on her finger with his little iron jaws.

"Ow!" She couldn't help herself. It hurt. Tears started in her eyes.

"Shh!" said the secretary.

"What is the meaning of this?" the man demanded.

How could she answer a question like that? How could you figure out the meaning of anything Mason did? "Sorry," was all she could manage. "Mason," she whispered fiercely into his ear, "I'm going to kill you when we get home. See if I don't."

Mason grinned.

The tears were coming down her cheeks—from anger as much as pain—while she gathered up the old, rumpled papers and banana peels and a spoiled orange. How in the world did this garbage get into a trash can in the office? What a school. What a terrible, old, smelly school and what horrible grown-ups in charge. She wasn't going to be able to stand it. She knew that already. She could stand a lot of things. She wasn't a baby, but some things were just too much to expect. She couldn't stand a school like this *and* being Mason Matthews's big sister. Mason should be in a special school for troubled children—or troubling children—or children who were nothing but trouble.

She sniffed back her tears. She didn't want the haughty secretary or the dreadful little man to see her cry. Even sitting down, the woman looked to be a head taller than the man who had come out of the office marked ASSISTANT PRINCIPAL. Vinnie didn't like people who were too tall or too short. She liked people to be normal sized. The secretary was tall and very skinny. She could slip right into the Addams family and feel right at home. While the little assistant principal—

The door of the principal's office opened. The assistant principal gave Vinnie one last disapproving look and disappeared behind his door. The window at the top of his door was covered on the inside with a venetian blind, the shutters closed.

Momma came out first and then Doctor Munchen. He was nervously (or so it seemed to Vinnie) ho ho hoing and patting Momma on the back. Momma was sort of squirming away from him and trying to smile bravely at the same time. "Well," she said, looking first at Mason, who was chomping away at his found gum, and then wrinkling her brow at Vinnie as if to say, Where did that gum come from? Vinnie shrugged, pretending not to know. She wasn't about to try to deal with Mason again.

"Mrs. Sealy, would you ask Mr. Clayton to send someone down for Lavinia?" She was so busy being mad that he'd called her "Lavinia" that for a moment she hadn't heard the rest of what he'd said.

Then she heard enough to realize that Momma was going to send her to a perfectly strange room in a perfectly terrible school all by herself. She looked at her mother in disbelief. Daddy would never have allowed such a thing. "Momma," she whispered.

"I know, sweetie. I'll try to meet your teacher later. First I have to see about Mason." She said it quietly in that

15

please-help kind of voice. What could Vinnie do? When the girl came down to escort her to the fourth-grade class, she just followed. She didn't even say good-bye to Momma or give Mason a threatening look. She squeezed her shoulders back tight and followed the girl out of the office, down the hall, and up two flights of dingy, old stairs to the top floor of the school.

Vinnie had seen a movie on TV once, one she knew she wasn't supposed to be watching. In it a woman had killed her husband. You couldn't blame her. He was cruel and beat her and threatened their little children. Anyhow, the police caught her and the courthouse where she was tried was just like Gertrude B. Somebody's Elementary School. Remembering, Vinnie knew how the woman had felt—the dark feeling of doom and despair, climbing step after dirty step up to the cold barn of a courtroom where she got sentenced to death in the electric chair. The movie even showed her dying. Vinnie shivered.

The girl hadn't said a word to Vinnie the whole way up to the fourth floor. Vinnie looked at the girl's back. She had smooth blonde hair above a pink T-shirt and blue jeans that fit beautifully. She was wearing nice sneakers, too. Vinnie knew they were brand-name sneakers—the right brand name. This school wasn't like Vinnie's old school in Washington. Here, there would be rich kids as well as ordinary kids and poor kids. Still, ordinary kids and poor kids were just as cliquey as rich kids. She would be left out of everything. There wouldn't be anybody like Shawna, who was always her best friend whatever happened.

"Are you coming in or what?" the girl was asking. Vinnie shoved her hair out of her face and walked into the weirdest-looking schoolroom she had ever seen. For one thing, everyone was sitting on the floor—well, on a

16

rug, but on the floor nevertheless. At first she didn't see any desks, then she realized that there were bunches of chairs with arms like desktops shoved against the walls. She looked for someone who might be the teacher. She had already decided that the teacher wasn't in the room, when someone got up off the floor. He wasn't too tall or too short—about the same size her father had been. He came over to the door, where Vinnie still stood.

"You must be Lavinia," he said. His voice was soft and not at all like a teacher's.

She nodded. She wanted to tell him that no one called her Lavinia except Grandma, who only did it when she was annoyed. But she felt shy, though not in a scared way—in a rather nice way. She didn't want this kind man to think she was criticizing him.

The teacher seemed to understand what she was thinking. "Is that what you want to be called? Lavinia?"

She shook her head. "Vinnie." Even though she whispered, the teacher heard her. "I'm Mr. Clayton, Vinnie," he said. "Welcome to 4C." He brought her to the top of the circle. The kids were staring at Vinnie, but she didn't mind as much as she thought she would. "Team," he said, "this is Vinnie Matthews. She's just moved here from—" He turned to Vinnie.

"Washington," Vinnie said softly.

"Washington. So she's a long way from home. It's up to us to make her feel welcome in Brownsville—especially at Gertrude B. Spitzer School—and most especially in the best class at the Spitzer School—" The class cheered. Mr. Clayton beamed at them.

"Now as you can see," he said, turning back to Vinnie, "we've rearranged things this morning. First, Heather, will you take Vinnie back to the cloakroom and help her find a cubby?" Heather nodded, none too pleased. "As soon as

17

you're set," Mr. Clayton said, smiling his wonderful smile at Vinnie, "you can join us in the circle."

The girl who had brought her up from the office nodded for Vinnie to follow. They wove around the end of some pushed-together chair desks through a door into a narrow sort of hallway at one end of the classroom. It had cupboards on either side. Inside each cupboard was a hook for a jacket or sweater and a shelf for a book pack and a lunch bag.

"I think this one's empty," Heather said. She seemed impatient to be rid of Vinnie and back to whatever was going on in the classroom.

Vinnie wanted to tell her to go on—that she could manage better without someone staring at her anyway. But she didn't feel like saying anything. The teacher expected Heather to be nice to Vinnie, and Heather hadn't said a single word that she didn't have to. She could just wait a minute. Vinnie put her brown lunch bag down and then turned her back on Heather and unzipped her jacket. She hung it on the hook. It slid off to the floor.

Heather humphed impatiently. Vinnie picked up the jacket and tried to arrange it more carefully. They could hear the class laughing at something Mr. Clayton had said. "Come on," said Heather. "We're missing the whole story." Without waiting, she hurried back into the classroom. By the time Vinnie got her jacket hung so it wouldn't fall off the hook and came alone into the room, Heather had melted into the closed circle.

Vinnie stood for a minute, not knowing how or if she should try to break into the group.

Mr. Clayton put his arm out as though to draw her into the circle. She went around to where he sat on the floor. "Push back a little, Brian," he said to the boy on his left. "Make way for Vinnie." He smiled up at her. Vinnie's face burned with pleasure. The teacher liked her. Even in this dumb, dirty old school, there was a teacher who was nice and who liked her. She sank to her knees beside Mr. Clayton.

"There," he said. "That's better. Now, where were we?"

3

As long as she was in the classroom, everything was fine at school. The playground and the lunchroom—they were the problems. That first day when the bell rang for morning recess, Mr. Clayton asked Heather to see that Vinnie knew where to go. Heather took her out to the playground and excused herself almost at once.

"Here. You can play on the swings or whatever you want. I got to see some people about a project we're working on. Okay?"

How could she say, No! You're supposed to take care of me. Don't leave me in this terrible place all by myself. She tried to smile. "Sure," she said.

That was the first time she noticed the tall girl. Sitting in the circle indoors, Vinnie had not really seen her. To tell the truth she had hardly paid attention to anyone except Mr. Clayton. On the playground, however, with no teachers around, the girl stood out like the golden arches at a McDonald's. She was tall. Maybe not six feet, though she seemed at least that to a girl like Vinnie, who scarcely scraped past four. Her hair was as long and stringy as Vinnie's, but it was black as Momma's funeral outfit. Her skin was the color of Ovaltine. Except for her warm tan complexion, everything else about the girl was almost witchlike. She was very thin, wearing a dress that swished around just a few inches above the ground. The other children on the playground, except for Vinnie and this tall, strange girl, were in jeans or neat, cotton slacks. Somehow the girl's swirling ankle-length dress made Vinnie self-conscious about the scuffed-up knees hanging out of her own too-short skirt.

The strangest thing about the girl was the flip-flops. She had feet as long and thin as Vinnie's whole arm, and instead of shoes or sneakers, she wore rubber flip-flops with bright orange thongs. Extending beyond the thongs were long, tan toes, the toenails slathered with bright purple polish.

Vinnie stared. All she could think of was Daddy singing:

> *"Herring box-es without tops-es*
> *Sandals were for Clementine."*

The flip-flop girl, again like Vinnie, was alone on the playground. While Vinnie gawked—she couldn't for the life of her pull her eyes away—the tall girl took a piece of chalk out of her pocket and calmly drew the outline of a hopscotch ladder. Then she pocketed the chalk, stepped out of the flip-flops, pitched a small stone into the first square, and began to hop, like a solo ballerina who has the whole stage to herself.

How did she dare go barefoot on a playground like

this? Vinnie didn't know whether to admire her for her bravery or despise her for her stupidity. There was broken glass and bits of metal on the playground. Flip-flops were dangerous enough, but barefoot . . .

How would anybody's mother let her come to school like that? Or grandmother? She wondered if the girl had any family, anyone to take care of her. She didn't look as though she had.

As Vinnie continued to stare at her, trying to imagine her life—she might well live in a gingerbread house in the woods as far as Vinnie could figure out—the tall girl gave Vinnie a glance out of the side of her dark brown eyes. She doesn't much like me watching her, thought Vinnie. Vinnie would have had a hard time keeping her eyes off the girl even if Heather and her friends had been bunched closely around her trying their best to make her feel happy and at home. But they were in a tight little knot on the far side of the jungle gym. Vinnie wondered about their "project." Boys? Every now and then, the little bunch of girls seemed to be sending a spy over to a group of boys playing basketball.

Vinnie watched the boys for a minute. She wanted to hoot. Not one of them, black or white, could make a basket. At her old school in Washington most of the boys were black and they were really good. Even fourth-graders practiced for hours every afternoon. They would have laughed these Brownsville boys off the court. And the court itself was just a bare metal ring mounted high over the same cracked concrete on which several yards away the flip-flop girl was patiently hopping out her solitary barefoot game.

A hundred years seemed to trudge past before the bell rang, but at last it did. The flip-flop girl pocketed her stone and slipped easily into her thongs. Then once again she caught Vinnie's stare. She tossed her hair proudly and ran to the door as quickly as though her feet had been encased in brand-name running shoes.

I bet she can play basketball, Vinnie thought, watching her run. "That's the bell," Heather said as she and her gang swept by. Vinnie reddened and trotted after them into the building and up those four long flights to where Mr. Clayton was waiting.

The first time Vinnie heard Mr. Clayton call the flip-flop girl by name she could hardly believe her ears. Loop. Like here we go loopedy loop. She must have heard wrong, but she hadn't. Later, among the Halloween drawings on the bulletin board, Vinnie spied a drawing of a huge jack-o'-lantern grinning evilly, and in the corner the name *Lupe M.* It took her a minute to put Lupe and loop together, but, of course, that must be how the flip-flop girl spelled her name.

As she sat all alone in the crowded lunchroom, Vinnie thought about the flip-flop girl. Lupe. What a strange name. Worse than Lavinia—far worse. Vinnie looked down at her hated leather shoes and cotton dress. They didn't seem so bad now, compared to what the flip-flop girl had to wear. The difference, she sighed, glancing at the chattering girls at the other end of the lunch table, the difference was that she cared what her name was and how she had to dress—the flip-flop girl didn't seem to. It bothered Vinnie that no one wanted to play with her. She hated to stand all alone on that awful playground trying to pretend she was doing something, when anyone could tell that she was standing there all by herself because no one would speak to her. The flip-flop girl just pulled her chalk and stone out of her pocket and played her solitary game of hopscotch as though no one else mattered—as though no one else even existed.

Vinnie found a trash basket and stuffed most of her

egg salad sandwich into it. Didn't Grandma know she hated egg salad? She bet Mason didn't have to eat egg salad for lunch. Vinnie went back to the table and sat down again. Maybe Heather or someone would look her way and ask her to join them. No one did. She folded up her empty brown paper bag carefully and stuck it into her jacket pocket. What if she waited a little longer? No one paid any attention, not even when she stood up and shoved her chair noisily against the lunch table.

Out on the playground, the flip-flop girl had already begun her game. Maybe Vinnie could go over and ask her—but no—how could she dare? It would be like asking the Wicked Witch of the West if you could play with her flying monkeys. She almost giggled. What would the flip-flop girl think if she could know what was going on inside Vinnie's head? Maybe she did know. Right at that minute she looked over at Vinnie. "Wanna play?" Although she spoke quietly, her voice was low and deep in her chest and carried all the way to where Vinnie was standing.

Should she say yes or no? She swallowed, nodded, and went toward the tall girl. The flip-flop girl hopped backward off the hopscotch ladder. "You need your own rock," she said in her soft, deep voice. She jerked her head toward the edge of the playground where some of the concrete had broken into small bits. Vinnie chose the smoothest piece she could find.

"Tomorrow," said the flip-flop girl, "bring a good rock from home. That stuff's no good." Lupe picked up her own stone. "We'll start over," she said and nodded at Vinnie, so Vinnie pitched her bit of concrete into the first square and hopped in, picked up the piece and hopped out again. Her leather shoes felt slick and pinchy, but it was better than being barefoot. Vinnie got the first and second squares easily, but when she threw her concrete marker toward the third square, it bounced out and away.

She stepped back and let the flip-flop girl have her turn. But Lupe never missed. She finished the entire game before Vinnie ever had another chance. The bell rang. "You'll do better with your own rock," the flip-flop girl said.

Vinnie nodded. She started toward the building. The flip-flop girl slipped into her thongs and ran to catch up with her. Vinnie didn't know what to do. If she played with the flip-flop girl, she was sure that Heather and the rest would never let her in their group. Still, it was better than standing around on the playground all alone, wasn't it? Maybe. Maybe not. She turned to wait for the flip-flop girl, but the tall girl had read her thoughts. She jogged straight past Vinnie into the school and up the steps, taking two at a time in her long stride.

If it hadn't been for Mason, Gertrude B. Spitzer School would have been almost bearable. Mr. Clayton made up for not having any real friends. He was the best teacher she'd ever had. Eating alone was always hard, but Lupe's hopscotch games made recess time pass by more quickly than Vinnie could have imagined. And while she was scared of the principal and especially the assistant principal, she hardly ever saw them.

She did have to see Mason. Every afternoon she had to go down to the ground-floor kindergarten room and collect Mason for the walk home. The principal had decided to put Mason in the small afternoon class so he could get more "individual attention." If any kid had plenty of individual attention, it was Mason Matthews. Momma and Grandma individual-attentioned him to death. Sometimes just thinking about Mason made Vinnie want to throw up. She wished she'd invented that no-talking trick. She could use a little individual attention every now and again.

The first day of school when she picked Mason up, the teacher was all smiles. Each day Mrs. Paxton's smile got tighter. That first day, a Monday, she had said, "Well, we had a good beginning, didn't we, Mason?" By Wednesday, she was saying, right in front of Mason, "He's such a strange little person." Vinnie had seen Mason's eyes light up. There was nothing he'd rather be than strange, unless it was a monster from outer space.

"He's not noisy," Mrs. Paxton had said on Thursday. "It's, well"—she gave Mason a quick look and then lowered her voice as though Mason were deaf as well as silent—"he races around the playground as though he's chasing ghosts. I find it a bit creepy."

Vinnie could have strangled the woman. Creepy was dangerously close to calling Mason an alien life-form. Mason's eyes were wide with delight. Couldn't the teacher tell that he was eating this up?

"Okay," Vinnie said. She didn't mean to be rude, she just needed to shut off this line of talk. "I'll tell Momma."

"Oh, I don't want to worry your poor mother."

Then just who did you want to worry? Vinnie should have sympathized with Mrs. Paxton. She knew how completely exasperating Mason could be—silently sabotaging everything a person might try to do. But Mrs. Paxton was supposed to be a *grown-up* for crying out loud, teachers were supposed to be experts on little kids. She ought to be able to handle one little five-year-old without complaining to his perfectly innocent sister, who wasn't even ten yet.

Once inside Mr. Clayton's classroom, however, Vinnie forgot to worry about how Mason was behaving down in the kindergarten room, forgot about the flip-flop girl, forgot about Heather and her gang. She even forgot sometimes that Daddy was dead.

On Friday that first week at Spitzer School, Mr. Clayton had a lesson on clouds. Other teachers would make you read about the weather in a book, but Mr. Clayton had them all crowd around the windows.

"Now," he said, "William, what does that cloud right there look like to you?"

"I dunno."

"Come on, William. You can't fool me." Mr. Clayton patted William's head affectionately. "I know there's a good brain in there between those handsome ears."

"Uh, uh," William stuttered, concentrating fiercely on the cloud. Arms were waving in the air like it was Flag Day, and a lot of people were making little Mr.-Clayton-look-at-me-I-know noises, but Mr. Clayton paid no attention to them. He was waiting patiently for William to think of something. Daddy had been like that, patient when someone was having trouble.

"Uh—streaks?" The class giggled. Mr. Clayton cocked his head, considering. "Blots and streaks?" William added, hopefully.

What a dumb answer, Vinnie thought, though she was careful not to giggle. She would have said the cloud looked like an angry old man with his mouth open, yelling, and his hair and beard blowing in the wind.

"A scientist would call that blot with streaks a cirrus cloud," Mr. Clayton was explaining. "It's very high—oh, three miles, maybe as much as eight miles above us here. And can you guess what it's made of?"

"Smoke?"

"Mist?"

"Ice," said Mr. Clayton. "Tiny little crystals of ice. It's so cold up there that all the moisture freezes."

"Wow," someone said as they all stared upward.

"It looks like Old Man Winter to me," Vinnie whispered into the quiet. "With wind blowing his hair and beard straight out."

"I like that," Mr. Clayton said and smiled down at her. "Why don't you do a poem about the cloud, Vinnie? It feels like a poem, don't you think?"

Vinnie nodded. Her ears burned with pleasure. During free reading that afternoon, she wrote two poems: one about a cloud to give to Mr. Clayton when she got up her nerve and one about Mr. Clayton that she would hide in her favorite book of poems and never show anyone.

When she got down to the kindergarten room after school to pick up Mason, he wasn't there. At first she panicked. Sometimes Mason just ran off from her without telling (of course, since he wouldn't talk) and she wouldn't know where to look for him. But Mrs. Paxton was all smiles. Grandma, she explained, had called to say he had a cold and she'd kept him home. Vinnie was as pleased as the teacher seemed to be. She had the whole walk home to think about clouds and Mr. Clayton.

She picked up a nice, long stick that was lying in the middle of the sidewalk and dragged it behind her. It made a comfortable scraping sound where the sidewalk was clear and a rustling noise through the fallen leaves. She loved the smell of the leaves. There were so many more leaves, so many more trees, here than in her neighborhood back home. She wasn't sure why she had thought Brownsville was so ugly at first. The leaves covered the sidewalks like variegated pieces of a picture puzzle, spilling over and decorating the street. They made a crispy, crunching sound under her shoes.

She came to a house surrounded by a freshly painted

picket fence. By pulling her stick across the white palings, she could make a tune quite different from the rustle and scrape of the sidewalk. Beyond the picket fence, she could see a high hedge. She was already wondering how her stick would sound on the hedge. She ought to write a poem about sticks scraping things. Was she the first person to think of writing such a poem?

She might become famous, oh, probably not while she was just a little kid, but when she was grown. There would be a ceremony like the Academy Awards for poets and she would win a prize. She began to act out the scene. No one was around so she did it aloud. She loved to play scenes out loud. They seemed so much more real than just inside her head.

"I am very honored to accept this award. I thank my mother. I hope she's proud of me. I only wish my father, who used to read poems to me, could be here, too. I especially want to thank my fourth-grade teacher, Mr. Wayne Clayton, who first recognized that in a shy little fourth-grader new to his class, there was buried deep down the poet who stands here tonight." She paused, wanting to make this a truly worthy speech. "Without his continued encouragement, and, yes, love, I would not be standing before you accepting this high honor. Mr. Clayton, please come forward. This honor rightfully belongs to you."

"Oh, no, Vinnie. May I still call you Vinnie? The award is yours. You earned it. I was only lucky enough to be around during the early blossoming of your talent. Can you imagine, ladies and gentlemen, the excitement? Here I am teaching nine- and ten-year-olds year after year— the same old thing and the same old dull kids, and then, suddenly, one day, this shy little person slips into my noisy class. There was something about her right from the first. 'Clayton,' I said, 'pay attention. You'll want to remember this day.' What a rare privilege to be able to be here tonight when the whole world recognizes what I saw so long ago in a fourth-grade classroom at Gertrude B. Spitzer Elementary School in Brownsville, Virginia!"

"Hey," a voice said from the far side of the hedge. "Who you talking to?"

Vinnie's stick clattered to the sidewalk. She stood frozen to the spot. Should she go forward to see who had caught her or turn and run back in the direction from which she'd come?

Too late. Lupe stepped out onto the sidewalk from the yard behind the hedge. She had a rake in her hands and a puzzled grin on her face.

"Who you talking to?" she asked again.

Vinnie made frantic motions behind her back as if to tell her secret companion to scram while there was still time. "I can't tell you," she said.

Lupe's eyebrow went up, her mouth still set in that infuriating grin.

"It's someone my mother won't let me play with."

"Oh," Lupe said in a way that made Vinnie sure she hadn't been fooled.

Her chest surged with fury. What right did Lupe have spying on people? Listening to their most private, secret thoughts? To calm herself, Vinnie leaned over and picked up her stick. With the tip, she carefully guided a brown oak leaf across the pavement. Her right hand was shaking so much, she had to help steady the stick with her left. Babies talked to themselves. Tiny children had imaginary playmates. Don't let her tell on me. Don't let her even know what I was doing. Maybe she really didn't hear any words—just some noises. Even if she heard a few words, she wouldn't know what Vinnie was saying, would she?

"Well," Vinnie said at last without looking up, "I got to go. My gran—my mother will be mad if I'm late."

"Sure," said Lupe, moving her big rake to one side to let Vinnie pass. "Sure."

Before Vinnie broke into a run, she stole a quick peek at Lupe's house. She remembered passing it before—huge and white with a big screened porch. There were giant oak trees in the yard. The house was ten times, well, maybe only twice as big as Vinnie's house, but the yard was at least ten times as big. And it had lots of grass under all those leaves, she was sure of that.

Vinnie didn't let herself think about what Lupe heard or didn't hear. She just began to run faster, and by the time she came to the tiny, baked bare yard of her own house, she was out of breath and her side ached.

Later that night, as Vinnie lay waiting for sleep, she began to wonder. If the flip-flop girl lived in a big house with a huge grassy lawn, why did she dress like a panhandler? And—Vinnie trembled at the thought—would she tell the kids at school that Vinnie talked to herself in the street like a crazy, homeless person? She flung herself over in bed, knocking Agnes to the floor. Straining, she leaned down over the side of the bed and grabbed up Agnes. She held her close. Was it weird that she still had to sleep with a doll?

Vinnie tried to think of "happy things." That was what Grandma said: "Just close the door to Old Man Unpleasantness and think of happy things." Happy, sappy. You couldn't just slam your brain like a back door.

4

Vinnie worried most of the weekend about seeing Lupe on Monday morning, but as Grandma said, "Don't waste your worry." Lupe wasn't even at school.

The first thing after the Pledge of Allegiance was announcements over the loudspeaker. Vinnie hardly ever listened. She was usually too busy watching Mr. Clayton. Today, while he was kneeling beside Eric Baines's desk, she noticed for the first time that he had a little bald spot on the back of his head. A bald spot? Could it mean that Mr. Clayton was old? She'd already decided that she would marry him.

Not now, of course, she wasn't that dumb. But someday. Oh, she was a little scrawny with muddy hazel eyes and long, wispy brown hair that wouldn't stay out of her face, but she would grow up. Someday she would be as beautiful as her mother. Her daddy had promised.

She'd be walking one spring afternoon in a lovely park—maybe Rock Creek Park in Washington since there was no lovely park in Brownsville—and she'd see him coming toward her, like in the perfume ads on TV.

"Mr. Clayton," she'd say, her voice soft and low, "you probably don't remember me, but—"

He'd look up. He'd been walking along rather sadly until that moment, but now he'd look up and say with surprise, "Vinnie Matthews! I hardly recognized you. You're all grown up and—and *so* beautiful." He would say this last in the same tone of voice that he'd said "It feels like a poem" the Friday before.

And she would be beautiful—totally beautiful. "I've never forgotten you," he would say. And later, after they were married, he would tell her how he had never given up hope that they would meet again.

In her mind she painted the house they would live in. Everyone, especially Mr. Clayton, marveled at her good taste. It was as big as Lupe's house and the lawn was a luxurious green with flowering trees in the spring and red maples ablaze in the fall. He, Wayne Clayton, had saved all his money for this dream house and now that he had found her again and —

"Vinnie." A harsh whisper popped her dreaming. She turned to face an annoyed Heather.

"You better listen to the announcements," Heather said. Her jaw was clenched, and she spat the words out between her teeth.

". . . graffiti on or near school property will be held accountable." Mr. Sharp, the assistant principal, often made threats during announcement time. But what did Heather think it had to do with her? Vinnie knew what graffiti was. Graffiti was when people scribbled their names or gang emblems or bad words on buses or walls. She certainly never did that. Graffiti was against the law, for heaven's sake.

The loudspeaker stopped squawking. Mr. Clayton was looking over the class to see who was there and who was absent. He smiled when he caught her eye. She felt warm all over. Was this the time to give him her poem? No, not while all the other kids were watching. Later. She could wait a minute until the classroom cleared at recess time. She blushed anyhow, just thinking about it.

He spoke, but not to her. "Has anyone seen Lupe Mahoney this morning?"

"She wasn't on the bus," William said.

"Hey, look," Bert yelled as loud as if he were calling for the ball on the playground. "Out the window."

Everyone rushed to the window without even waiting for permission. Vinnie was the last to get there and had to wriggle through to see at all. But what a sight to see! Coming down the sidewalk toward the front of the school was someone pushing a wheelbarrow, and in the wheelbarrow was the largest pumpkin you could imagine. It was four or five times as wide as the person pushing the barrow and almost as tall as it was wide.

"It's Lupe!" someone yelled, as the tiny person four floors below began to struggle to heft the huge pumpkin out of the wheelbarrow.

"William—Bert—" Mr. Clayton sounded like a top sergeant. "Get down there and give her a hand. What a pumpkin! Wow!" The top sergeant had turned into a five-year-old. Vinnie's own excitement soured a little. Why should Mr. Clayton sound so thrilled over a pumpkin? One that Lupe had brought?

The class watched out the window, jostling one another for better views until they saw William and Bert banging out the center door and racing down the long front steps. "Yeah!" Eric Baines yelled. "The cavalry to the rescue!" All the boys whistled and cheered. When William and Bert arrived at the wheelbarrow, Lupe at first pushed them away from the pumpkin. Now the girls cheered. The two boys looked up toward the window as though appealing for help from above. Mr. Clayton raised the window and stuck his head out. "Teamwork!" he yelled down at the three of them.

Whoever heard of a teacher yelling out of a school window? Immediately, Lupe stopped struggling and elbowing the boys away. The three of them each put their hands under a different part of the giant pumpkin. They leaned their chests against the fat orange belly and began awkwardly to climb the steps. William was going up backward, but the pumpkin was so large that none of them could see where they were going. They kept screaming to one another, and every two or three steps they'd stop and rearrange themselves.

Before they got all the way up to the landing in front of the door, the main door had opened. "Eek!" someone said softly. "Rat patrol!" Mr. Sharp emerged from the building. No one at the window could hear what he was saying, but they all knew it was not pleasant. The three pumpkin bearers shifted their weight nervously as they stood listening.

"I'd better go down." Mr. Clayton loosened himself from the knot around the window.

They watched, hardly daring to breathe, until they saw his blond head come out of the front door. A few words passed between him and Mr. Sharp. Strain as they could, no one—not even Jake, who was leaning so far out of the open window that Heidi grabbed his T-shirt to hold him back—could hear a word.

Soon, though it seemed like ages, the whole party disappeared into the building. The class drifted back toward their own desks, though no one wanted to sit down.

"Wonder what Rat Face was doing out there?" Jake said. It was what everyone was wondering.

"Nothing good, that's for sure," Gary muttered. Gary was famous for having survived the school record of sessions spent behind Mr. Sharp's venetian blind–shrouded door.

Then they heard laughter and noisy shouts of directions and "Sh—sh—keep it down, team" from the stairwell. They rushed to the door and flung it open, pouring out to help the pumpkin bearers the last few feet of their journey.

"No, no," Mr. Clayton shouted, "if you really want to help, get out of the way. No, wait, you two"—pointing his nose at Gary and Jake—"go get the wheelbarrow and put it in the teachers' room. I wouldn't want anyone to pinch that off the street."

Huffing and tugging and laughing, the crew got the huge pumpkin through the classroom door and lifted it high enough to plunk it down—"Careful! It's fragile, folks!"—on Mr. Clayton's desk, scattering yesterday's math papers like leaves to the autumn wind.

Heather ran forward and picked the papers up. Vinnie pushed her hair out of her face and wished she hadn't hung back, for Heather was rewarded with a beaming smile and a "Thanks, Heather, that was thoughtful."

Mr. Clayton spent the rest of the day totally on pumpkins. There was no chance to give him her cloud poem at recess. He forgot all about recess. He sent Heidi down to the nurse's room to borrow the scales so they could weigh the pumpkin—97 pounds, 2 ounces. They measured it. Since no one had a tape measure, they used a string, which they then laid on the yardstick to translate into feet and inches—8 feet, 8¾ inches around the middle.

They tried to calculate how many pumpkin pies could

be made from this single pumpkin—though who, asked Mr. Clayton, would waste such a glorious spheroid ("Look it up, Ashley, it's in the dictionary!") on pies?

At story time, instead of the book he had been reading, Mr. Clayton told them "The Legend of Sleepy Hollow." It frightened Vinnie and made her want to stop her ears, but how could she? Mr. Clayton was having a wonderful time making all the scary sounds and voices and turning his own warm smile into a leering jack-o'-lantern. She was shaken seeing him so evilly transformed.

"Tomorrow I'll bring knives to carve it," he said. "Who can bring aprons and newspapers?" Nearly every hand went up. "And we'll save the seeds. Divide them up and you all can take some home to dry and toast. They're delicious and nutritious. See, they rhyme! Delicious and nutritious!" He looked around for approval. Everyone giggled obediently except Vinnie. It bothered her that Mr. Clayton was acting so much like a kid.

"For today," he continued, "we'll have a contest to design a face for our noble friend here. And a name contest. Any vegetable this noble should have a name."

"It already has a name." Everyone turned. It was the seldom-heard voice of Lupe herself. She had stood up and was talking to Mr. Clayton as though none of the rest of them existed.

Mr. Clayton beamed at her. "What is its name, Lupe?" he asked in his gentlest voice.

Lupe's tan face flushed a dusky rose, but she kept her eyes fixed on the teacher's face. "Patrick," she said steadily. "Patrick Mahoney."

A hush fell over the class. They stopped staring at Lupe and looked at one another. "Sure," said Mr. Clayton, and this time his face and neck turned pink. "Patrick Mahoney, it is. May we call it Pat for short?"

Lupe nodded and sat down. Who on earth was Patrick Mahoney? Vinnie realized that she was the only person in the room who didn't know. But who could she ask? Everyone knew and they also knew that it was very weird that Lupe wanted the pumpkin to have that name. Spooky even, like "The Legend of Sleepy Hollow" or something.

The moment passed. Soon everyone was busily drawing a design for the pumpkin face contest—everyone except Vinnie. She wasn't good at drawing. There was no way she could win the contest and get Mr. Clayton's praise and smile and undivided attention. Hers would just be one of the dumb pictures no one gave a second look at. Something poked the insides of her throat. How dare Lupe make such a fuss—turn the whole class upside down—with her stupid pumpkin? Suddenly Vinnie realized she hated pumpkins. Jack-o'-lanterns weren't fun, they were scary. She would just as soon never see another one. She'd never liked the taste of pumpkin—wasn't it just a big squash? Even in pies, no amount of brown sugar ever disguised the squashy flavor.

When Mr. Clayton came by her seat, her paper was perfectly blank. "I can't draw," she said, hearing the whine in her voice.

He raised his eyebrows, opened his mouth, but instead of protesting, he said, "How about a poem, then? You like poems, don't you?"

"Not about pumpkins."

Mr. Clayton heard the pouting tone in her voice. He cocked his head to one side, but he didn't say anything—just moved on to Brian, who was filling his large sheet of drawing paper with a face that was all orange teeth and wicked eyes.

She wanted to call the teacher back and say she hadn't

meant to be such a baby, that of course she would write him a poem or draw a picture or do anything he wanted. But it was too late. Everything was spoiled. The day that had started in a wonderful dream had ended in a wretched frenzy over an overgrown pumpkin head.

Dragging Mason home, she couldn't shake her mood, not even when instead of Grandma it was Momma who met them at the door. She had already changed out of her white uniform into a pair of slacks and Daddy's old plaid jacket. Momma was always wearing Daddy's clothes. Vinnie wished there were something of his she could wear, but of course she couldn't because all of his things were too big for her.

"I came home early," her mother said, after she'd sent Mason into the kitchen for Grandma to try to get a snack down him. "I came home a little early, so you and I could—" she lowered her voice so Mason couldn't overhear. "It's nearly Halloween and I heard about this place where you can get pumpkins cheap. Let's just you and me go and get one. We can surprise Mason."

"I hate pumpkins," Vinnie said, the echo bouncing around her head.

"You won't have to eat it, promise. Oh, come on, Vinnie, just for the ride. Just the two of us?"

Vinnie looked up. Her mother was smiling her little, crooked "help me" smile. Vinnie sighed. "Okay," she said.

On the drive she almost forgot the day at school. Momma was humming and squinting her eyes against the sun, which was bright and orange. "Just like a pumpkin," her mother said.

"Where are we going?"

"I'm not sure." Her mother laughed and glanced over at her. "Worried?"

Vinnie shook her head. Being with her mother—just the two of them together—how long had it been? No Grandma chattering away. No silently demanding Mason. "It's fun," Vinnie said. "Like an adventure."

Momma reached over and patted her on the knee. "That's my girl." It was what Daddy used to say to her.

"A woman who came to the office told me about this place. It's sort of a pumpkin farm built on an abandoned garbage dump, so the ground is great for growing things. They sell their pumpkins cheap, too." She laughed and lowered the visor against the sun. "And you know me for cheap."

Vinnie giggled.

"She said it was west of town just by the old railroad trestle."

"How far out of town?"

"Well, Myra's not big on detail. She said about a half mile. But I'm sure we've gone more than a mile already." Her mother glanced at the odometer and began to slow down. "Help me look for the sign. There's supposed to be a sign."

"Which side?"

"She said left, but she looked at her wedding ring before she said it, so I'm not sure we can trust— There it is." Her mother hit the brakes, bouncing Vinnie against the seat belt. "Sorry. See? There it is."

On the other side of the road was a table made from an old door that had been ripped from its frame—the hinges were still attached. It was resting on a pair of unpainted sawhorses. A crudely painted sign was nailed to a stake stuck in the grass beside the table. "Pumpkins $1 up," it read. But there were no pumpkins to be seen.

In fact, Vinnie could see nothing either on the table or behind it. The land beyond the table simply dropped off.

Her mother was unfastening her seat belt and getting out of the car. "Look at that, will you?"

Vinnie loosened her belt and crawled over the gear stick to the driver's side to get out. The view was something from *The Wizard of Oz*. Beyond the table where the land had seemed to drop off, there was a deep crevasse, like a giant bowl, carpeted with pumpkin vines—great lush tangles of deep green vines splashed with blobs of orange. The field—you could hardly call it a patch—stretched from the foot of the high, curving railroad bridge at the western end, the full length of the crevasse. There was no other person in sight.

"I guess we got here too late," Vinnie said. She didn't know why she was trembling.

"Oh, no. Not after we've come all this way. Let's just go down and ask at the house."

"What house?" But as soon as she asked, she saw it—a tiny, unpainted shack, not far from the long metal leg of the trestle, leaning into the opposite hill.

Her mother had already started down the steep path. "We're too late," Vinnie called after her. "Let's go home—please."

"It'll be an adventure, just like you said," her mother called back over her shoulder.

What could Vinnie do but follow, half sliding, half stumbling down toward the green-and-orange jungle?

They wound their way through the bottom of the bowl toward the little house. It looked as though some giant hand had slapped it back into the hill under the threatening skeleton of the trestle. The setting sun danced on the golden balls on the nearer side of the field, but as they got closer to the house, they were engulfed in the shadow of the trestle and the hill. Vinnie felt goose bumps crawling up her arms.

"Chilly out of the sun, isn't it?"

Vinnie nodded. Her mother waited now until she had caught up, then reached toward her and took her hand as if she'd been Mason. Her mother smiled. "Peter, Peter, pumpkin eater . . ." she began.

Vinnie squeezed her mother's hand. She didn't feel nine anymore. She felt younger than Mason. She remembered the time Daddy had taken her to the zoo in Washington. She was so excited. She loved animals. She knew the name and the sound of every animal in all her books. Of all the stuffed toys she'd had when she was little, she had loved her bear the best.

But when she saw those huge polar bears with dirty white fur and enormous teeth, she had screamed. Not once, but over and over until Daddy had given up and taken her home again without even seeing the monkeys. She had never gone back to the zoo again. Now she never would.

They had begun to climb out of the pumpkin field up the short slope to the house. The shack was dark. No light shone from the small, high windows. "No one's home," Vinnie whispered. "Let's go." She said this, even though she was sure she'd seen someone moving at one of the windows.

"There's smoke, see?" her mother answered. The path narrowed and she let go of Vinnie's hand. Vinnie walked almost on Momma's heels the last steps to the stoop. Her mother turned and mouthed the word "adventure" before lifting her hand to knock on the splintery door. "We've come to buy a pumpkin," she called out cheerily.

The door opened a crack. At once Vinnie knew. She knew exactly who lived in this strange house. She should have known all along. The big house with all the trees in the yard had fooled her. See, there was an orange thong.

She followed the narrow opening up until she saw in the crack a glimpse of Lupe's dark face and proud, flashing eyes.

"We've come to buy a pumpkin," her mother said again.

Lupe gave them both a glance but made no sign that she had ever seen either of them before. "I sold all the cut ones," she said. "It's late." Vinnie could see a dim light behind Lupe now. Someone was calling to Lupe from inside. Vinnie couldn't understand the words. Not a mother's voice, surely, maybe a grandmother's. Lupe closed the door to a sliver hardly wider than a hopscotch line.

"I know it's late," Momma said. "I'm sorry. But we weren't sure of the way. It took us longer than we thought."

Lupe disappeared and then came out, carrying a huge machete. She slipped through the narrow opening and closed the door quietly behind her, ignoring the voice calling to her from inside. "What size?" she asked Momma, not even seeming to notice Vinnie—treating her the way she did Heather and the others on the playground.

"As large as we can get for two dollars," Momma said brightly, glancing nervously at the dangerous-looking blade.

"It's my pop's," Lupe said, reading minds as usual.

She led the way back into the field. It was already twilight there, but she left the path and jumped surely and gracefully into the tangle. With a quick flick of her wrist, she loosed a pumpkin, which she brought back on the palm of her left hand. It was a normal jack-o'-lantern-sized pumpkin, a tiny moon compared to the earth-sized one she had brought to school.

"It's perfect!" Momma said, holding out two dollars. "Want to carry it?" she asked Vinnie.

Vinnie nodded and, without looking at Lupe, took the pumpkin from her outstretched hand.

They were nearly up the slope to the car before either Vinnie or her mother spoke. "What an unusual girl," her mother said at last. "I wonder how old she is."

It would have been easy to say "My age" or "She's in my class" or "She's the only one who will have anything to do with me at recess . . ." But Vinnie said nothing. Was she ashamed? Afraid? It was hard to know. Whatever it was, she couldn't seem to tell her mother that Lupe Mahoney was the closest thing she had to a friend in Brownsville.

"Come on, sweetie pie, just a little trim."

Grandma had caught her lying on her bed, daydreaming over the book she was reading.

"No!" Vinnie jumped off her bed and headed for the stairs, Grandma in hot pursuit, the scissors held high like a dagger.

"You're starting to look like a wet mop on a cold floor! Lemme just get the bangs."

"No! I said no! Don't touch me!" Vinnie's hair was too long. Nobody knew it better than she did. It hung in her face and she was always having to push it out of her eyes. But she wasn't about to let Grandma cut it. "Momma!" she bleated, running down the hall to the kitchen, where her mother was deep in soapsuds at the sink, Mason holding her by the sweater and sucking his thumb as though he were absorbing nourishment from her body.

"My gracious, Vinnie. What on earth?"

"Grandma . . . Grandma . . ." She was panting as though a tiger were on her tail. "Grandma's trying to get me."

"Oh, for goodness' sake. Nobody's trying to get you."

But there was Grandma standing in the kitchen doorway, red-faced and out of breath, her long-bladed, black-handled scissors still held up high. When she saw Momma staring at her, she lowered her arm. "Grace. The child needs a haircut. Aren't you shamed as I am to see her going to school looking like something the cat dragged in from a hailstorm?"

"It's all right, Mother Matthews." Momma put her arm around Vinnie, making her feel protected. "I'll take her somewhere to get it done. Soon as I get paid."

"It's a waste of money, Gracie. I always cut everyone's hair. I'm real good at it. No point paying someone."

"Maybe not. But, well, Vinnie's at that age . . ." No one would ever know what "that age" was because Grandma shrugged her shoulders in disgust and walked away. Vinnie could feel her body shaking against Momma's. She felt like a baby—like a Mason—which made her angry.

"She scared me . . . "

"Shh. It's all right. No one's going to cut your hair unless you want them to."

She wanted to thank Momma for taking her side—for protecting her—but she couldn't seem to say anything. It all seemed so silly. She wasn't some crazy little mixed-up kid like Mason. And Grandma, she knew quite well, was not some kind of ax murderer. All she needed to do was say quietly and firmly to Grandma that—that what? She wanted to put her arms around Momma and cry and cry. Not for any particular reason. Just cry until all the lumps and sharp points inside her throat melted and ran out with the tears. But she couldn't squeeze a single teardrop.

"Want to help me?"

Vinnie nodded, swallowing hard. She got a dishtowel from the drawer and began to dry, trying her best to ignore Mason, who had latched himself even more tightly onto Momma—like one of those ticks that give you a disease.

"I wish Daddy were here, don't you?" She felt daring, bringing up the subject of Daddy.

Her mother didn't answer. Vinnie stopped drying. "Don't you?" she asked again.

"Yes," her mother said in a tiny, strangled voice.

Vinnie looked at her. Was she going to cry? Half of Vinnie wanted Momma to scream and yell and beat her fists in the soapsuds. But Momma didn't. She stood very still, gripping the side of the sink, working her face around until she got it under control. "Yes," she said again in a voice as quiet as death, "I always wish he were here."

The next day at school her hair nearly ran her crazy. She kept shoving it off her face. Sometimes she felt as though she were looking at the world through a thick veil of spider web—a thick, scratchy veil that made her blink and feel cross-eyed.

It was math-test day. Math tests were scary enough, but today she couldn't make her way through the jungle of her hair to the page on the desk. She kept pushing at her hair, remembering Lupe cutting the pumpkin vine with her huge machete. She needed a machete herself. Whenever she leaned over to read through the problem, her hair fell back again, thicker and harder to see through than before.

She wanted to scream. It was Grandma's fault. If she hadn't sneaked up on Vinnie with those horrible long scissors . . . Everything was so wrong now. Used to be Sheila, who was a certified beautician and lived in the apartment upstairs, would come down and cut everyone's hair in exchange for Momma's baby-sitting her two-year-old on the days Sheila went to work in the beauty parlor.

Sheila was what Momma called a "real artist." She always brought down her delicate silver-colored scissors, and she never yanked your hair or jabbed your neck by mistake. She also cut Daddy's hair. Even when he was sick, he would joke with Sheila. The treatments made him nearly bald, but Sheila would trim the few thin strands he had left. "It's straight as a stick, Sheila," he'd say. "What about a little body wave?"

"Oh, Wes," she'd say. "If you make me laugh, I'm liable to slice a piece out of your ear." Then she'd laugh until her fat tummy shook. They'd all laugh. Even Mason and Sheila's baby, April, though April and Mason didn't catch on. They just laughed because everyone else did.

The bell rang. Vinnie looked up in alarm. People were passing in their math papers and getting in line for recess. The time couldn't be up. She'd hardly done half the problems. The class filed out. Vinnie just sat there.

Wrong. She erased the same spot for the umpteenth time. Straight through the paper. She tried to smooth the hole with the heel of her hand. She would not cry. She jammed her hair back behind her ears and tried again.

Mr. Clayton watched the last child out and then came over to Vinnie's desk. She tried to cover her smudged, eraser-worn paper with her left hand. "I haven't quite finished."

"Take your time," he said. "It's not meant to be a race."

A wave of love swept over Vinnie. What a wonderful, kind teacher. He was just like Daddy.

He walked to his desk and then came back. "Here," he said, his big, freckled hand putting something down beside her paper. "I try to be prepared for all emergencies."

When he lifted his hand, Vinnie saw a card—like the ones at Woolworth—with two red plastic bows attached.

"Barrettes," he said, as though she might need help figuring it out. "They're on permanent loan."

She was too astonished to speak.

"A present," he said, smiling his lovely smile. He had perfect teeth, except for one little slightly crooked eyetooth. "My compliments." He went back to his own desk, sat down, and began marking papers.

With shaking hands, Vinnie took the barrettes off the cardboard and, pulling back her wayward bangs, fastened first the left side and then the right in place.

Mr. Clayton looked at her. "Very nice," he said.

She glowed, patting the little red bows, which some people might think were babyish, but which at this moment Vinnie thought were the loveliest hair ornaments ever invented. Then, remembering the test, she went back to work. It was as though the barrettes were sending secret messages into her brain. The problem that had sent her eraser clear through the paper was laughably easy now. She moved through the rest of the problems, not exactly like magic, but close enough.

The next time Mr. Clayton paused in his marking, she caught his eye and said, "I only got one more."

"Fine," he said. "No rush. I'm not going anywhere."

When she took up the paper, she wanted to thank him for the present, for the time, for making everything okay, but she couldn't figure out how to say it all without sounding silly. "You want me to wash the board or something?" she asked, touching the left barrette with the tips of her fingers.

"Not right now, but thanks for asking." He nodded at the barrette. "Feel better?"

"Yessir. Thank you."

He glanced up at the clock. "You've got just about enough time to make a pit stop before the bell rings."

He meant she should leave. She hated to, but she did. Even though she didn't have to go to the bathroom, she went anyway. That tiny stall was the only private place in her life anymore. It didn't matter that her feet showed at the bottom and she couldn't talk out loud to herself, still there was no Mason—no Grandma—no Lupe. She could sit there and think her own thoughts.

Today, however, there was no one else in the whole bathroom, so she stood at the mirror and arranged and rearranged her new barrettes, putting the sharp metal clasp deep into her hair to see just how much it could hold. She wondered if anyone would ask where they had come from and what to say if they did. But no one asked either in the bathroom or later in class.

Lupe might have noticed. Walking past Vinnie on the way to her own desk, she seemed to glance at Vinnie's head. She may have even started to say something, but just then the hall door opened, and the assistant principal stomped into the room. "Lupe Mahoney! To my office. At once."

Everyone's head snapped up as though they'd heard a shot. Only Mr. Clayton moved. In one swift swoop, he was out of his desk, his nose in Mr. Sharp's face.

His voice was very low, but there wasn't a soul in the room who missed a word. "May I see you outside, sir?" He didn't actually grab the AP, though several people swore later that he had, but he maneuvered him into the hall as quickly as if he had him by the neck. The class held their collective breath.

"May I ask, sir, what this is about?"

"I know you feel sympathetic towards the girl, Mr. Clayton, and that's very admirable, but I'm responsible for discipline in this school, and I will not have graffiti on the playground . . ."

"For pity sake, man, it's just hopscotch. Kids have been drawing hopscotch squares on playgrounds forever. Nobody in their right minds would call it—"

"You weren't out there today, Clayton. Obviously."

"I was grading math papers—"

"Three-foot-high letters in that hideous orange chalk."

"Oh?"

"You wouldn't know what it said?"

"No, as you observed, I wasn't outside today."

"'Congratulations . . .'"

"What?"

"That's what she wrote. 'Congratulations, Mr. C.'"

"Well, I'll be damned. How did she know?"

"That is not at issue. The issue is . . ."

The end of recess bell jangled, and when the reverberations had died, there was silence. Strain as they did toward the door, they could hear nothing but the loud tick of the classroom clock and the muffled sounds of traffic from the street below.

At last they gave up listening. The bell had blotted out the conversation in the hall. Gary dared peek out the door. "They're gone," he reported in a loud whisper.

Now all eyes turned on Lupe. She ignored them, moving down the aisle past Vinnie, crossing the back of the room, and plunking down in her seat at the rear of the classroom.

It was a signal for all of them to sit down. Some kids cleared their throats, and you could hear the occasional buzz of a whisper, but mostly, they waited.

51

"Will Lupe Mahoney report to the office?" They all jumped at the blared command from the intercom.

Lupe got up, carefully straightened her desk, and walked to the door. She closed it after herself, holding it to make sure it didn't slam.

The class erupted. Vinnie's head was spinning. No one spoke directly to her, so she was left to sort out snatches of conversation from around her. But the question that she didn't want put into words, that sat like cold beans at the pit of her stomach, was: Congratulations for what?

Finally, Mr. Clayton returned, followed by Lupe, who walked quickly back to her desk. She looked her usual self, unruffled, a bit arrogant. His face, however, was a furious red. The words "Day-Glo orange" came into Vinnie's head. The teacher didn't ask them to quiet down. He didn't have to. They might have been a field of stones for all the noise they made.

"I think we'll do free reading for the next forty-five minutes," he said. "Anyone who needs a book can get one from the shelf or take a library slip."

He went over to Lupe, whispering something in her ear. She got up, fetched her jacket, and left the room. By the end of free reading, she was back in her place, her dark head bent over her book.

When the class went out on the playground after lunch, there were no graffiti to be seen—just a large, rather pinkish smear on the concrete in the area where Vinnie and Lupe usually played hopscotch. Vinnie didn't want to play hopscotch that day, and Lupe didn't suggest it. She didn't even draw the squares.

That night Vinnie overheard Momma and Grandma talking in the kitchen. She was supposed to be upstairs, but she'd come down to complain that Mason had left his bed to get into Momma's again. It was against the rules.

Momma had told him repeatedly that he had to stay in his own bed.

"I keep thinking about that strange girl," Momma was saying.

"What strange girl?"

"Where we bought the pumpkin the other day."

"Oh the Mahoney girl."

"You know her?"

"I know *about* her," Grandma said. "Her father brought her down here last year. From someplace up north—Boston, New York. I forget."

"To that dreadful place?"

"He was running from the law." She gave a funny, abrupt laugh. "Can you imagine? You'd think he'd know the first place they'd look for him was his mother's house."

"But why did he bring the girl?"

"What else could he do? He'd killed her mother. She was Mexican or Puerto Rican or something. They say he was jealous. Oh, he denied it, but there didn't seem much doubt."

"Poor child."

Lupe? Lupe's father a murderer? Patrick Mahoney. No wonder everyone thought it was weird when Lupe said that was the name of the pumpkin. Chills went through Vinnie, starting with her feet. They felt like chunks of ice on the cold hardwood floor of the hallway. She turned around and tiptoed back upstairs to her bed. No wonder Lupe was so strange. No wonder no one liked her.

Except Mr. Clayton. He ought to be careful. Of course the AP was upset. Teachers shouldn't make a murderer's child their pet. Vinnie needed to be more careful herself. Bad blood. No. Bad seed. Criminals had bad children. She knew that much. Everyone ought to watch out.

At recess the next day Vinnie hugged the wall of the building. If she stayed in the shadow, maybe Lupe wouldn't see her. She had decided definitely not to be friendly to Lupe. Where was Lupe, anyway? The pinkish area of concrete that used to be the hopscotch game was empty. Maybe she was spending recess inside with Mr. Clayton. It wasn't fair. Mr. Clayton shouldn't give one kid so much more attention than he did the others. Besides, he'd get himself in more trouble with the assistant principal if he wasn't careful.

"Like some pumpkin seeds?"

Vinnie jumped. Lupe was standing right behind her, holding out a little brown bag. "I toasted them like Mr. C said. They're good."

"No. Thanks." Should she walk away?

"Oh, go on. I don't have some contagious disease."

Vinnie went red. How could the flip-flop girl read her

mind? She took a small tan seed from the bag and put it in her mouth. It tasted of butter and salt—sort of like popcorn but more, well, seedy. She sucked it, not knowing how to eat a seed.

"Just crack it open with your teeth." Lupe demonstrated. "And then spit the cover out." She did so, right on the playground surface.

Vinnie looked down, horrified.

Lupe grinned. "You're right. Not a great idea." She stooped down and picked up the spittle-covered hull. "I'm in trouble enough, right?"

Vinnie chewed the seed, hull and all, and swallowed. It stuck a little going down.

Lupe leaned her tall frame back against the building. "Sorry about the hopscotch," she said. "I guess I messed up—doing that sign."

Vinnie wanted to ask the meaning of the sign—the graffiti that had brought the wrath of the AP upon Lupe, but she didn't.

"My pop didn't do it, you know."

"I—I—" Vinnie wanted to pretend she didn't know, but it was too late.

"He—my pop—had this friend. At least he thought he was a friend. He pretended to be friends. Then the guy did this total flip-flop . . ." At the word, Vinnie started. "You know," Lupe continued, "he"—and here she flipped her hands over—"he was all pals and then when, when, well, afterwards, he told the police all these lies . . ."

Vinnie turned away. She didn't want to know about Lupe's father and his flip-flop friend.

"I heard *your* father's dead. That's too bad."

"It's okay." She didn't want to talk to Lupe Mahoney about Daddy.

"Your real name Vinnie? Or you got a nice name?"

"Lavinia." She cleared the cobweb from her throat. "I like Vinnie better."

"Really?" Shaking her head, Lupe took out another pumpkin seed and cracked it between her teeth. She offered the bag to Vinnie, but Vinnie shook her head. "I like my real name best. Maria Guadalupé." The words rolled off her tongue like an exotic melody. "But nobody calls me by it. Even my pop just called me Lupe, not Lupay." She took the hull out of her mouth and held it between her fingers. "Mom said, 'Don't mind, he's Irish. What do he know?' So I don't mind." She shrugged.

Vinnie didn't watch Lupe eating her seeds, but she could feel the tall girl standing beside her—a girl her own age whose mother was dead—killed dead—and a father in jail for it. She wanted to say something, like "That's too bad," but no words came out.

"Sure you don't want some seeds?"

"No. Thanks anyway."

School was quiet that day. Even Mr. Clayton seemed subdued. Only Patrick Mahoney grinned, his enormous snaggle-toothed face mocking them all.

At the final bell, Vinnie gathered her things into her book pack and started for the kindergarten room. Going to fetch Mason meant two flights to the main floor of being jostled, pushed, and yelled at; then another flight to the ground floor, making her way down the length of the hall against the stream of children rushing and pushing to get out of the building. By the time she got to the door of the kindergarten room, there was no Mason to be seen. Vinnie stuck her head into the room. No Mrs. Paxton either.

She was tempted—oh, so tempted—to race through the hall and zoom out the door, free for one glorious afternoon from his climbing every fence, dawdling on every sidewalk, sitting down in the middle of streets when she wanted him to hurry, and running away when she was too tired to chase him.

With a sinking heart, she climbed back up to the main floor and trudged toward the dreaded office. Just as she'd feared, there was Mrs. Paxton and the AP with Mason between them. Each of them had a hand on one of his shoulders as they came out the office door. She froze in place. The grown-ups stood talking over Mason's head, not letting go for a minute. What had he done now?

She waited there so long that the last of the departing students had banged out the doors. There was no one to hide behind. Her feet felt like cement blocks as she dragged them toward the trio in front of the office. One last someone, racing to be free from school, clipped her shoulder as he sped past, half spinning her around. She almost cried out in pain. Tears sprang to her eyes. The boy never turned around. Maybe Mr. Sharp would stop him and give him fits for running in the halls. But Mr. Sharp didn't even notice—he was yelling at Mason. She shifted her backpack to the other shoulder and tramped grimly on, blinking back the tears.

"There she is." The AP had spotted her. "You're the sister, aren't you?" As though it were some kind of crime to be kin to Mason. She couldn't help being Mason's sister. She sure hadn't chosen to be.

"Talking sense to this child is like plowing sand." She had a wonderful picture of a plow running through the Sahara Desert—although that might be fun. Mason was not fun, whatever he was. "I want you to tell him," the AP continued, "and I want you to make it perfectly clear, we will not tolerate this behavior."

Vinnie supposed she ought to ask what Mason had done, but she was afraid that if she opened her mouth she might just say something she'd be sorry for later.

"He spit, *spit* into the juice cups at snack time. Into all twenty cups."

"He made the other children cry," Mrs. Paxton added.

Dweebs, thought Vinnie. Why didn't the other kids just sock him? Made them cry, did he? Like Georgie Porgie? Gimme a break.

The AP turned to Mason again. "What have you got to say for yourself, young man?"

Mason wasn't even looking at the AP. He was staring up at the high ceiling of the hall as though studying the cracks in the plaster.

Mr. Sharp took Mason by the shoulders and turned him around. "Look at me while I'm speaking to you."

Mason shook himself, wriggled out of the AP's grasp, and headed for the far door.

"Come back here, young man!" Mason didn't turn a hair. He just kept walking.

"You. Go get him and bring him back here," the AP ordered Vinnie.

"Yessir," Vinnie mumbled, but she didn't start for the door. Who was she to make Mason obey? He'd never obeyed her in his life. She was torn. Should she chase after Mason or stay and try to explain that it was useless? Neither would work, but she chose to chase. Anything to get away. She ran as fast as she could down the hall, the books in her pack thumping painfully against her shoulder blades.

She caught up with Mason before he reached the end of the corridor. "Please, Mason," she begged. "You got to go back."

He paused momentarily, gave her an unblinking stare, and then marched on like a little robot, untouched by human pleas.

"I mean it, Mason. That guy is really strict. He'll get you if you don't straighten out. Just come back and tell him you're sorry." Stupid idea. "You don't have to say anything. Just look sorry—just a *teeny* bit sorry. You don't need to say a word."

Mason kept walking.

"Please. For me. Just this once. I don't want to be in trouble and they'll blame me. I'm supposed to be responsible. I'm supposed to make you behave. Dumb idea, huh?"

He pushed through the heavy fire door. She caught the door as it swung back and ran past him down the flight of steps that led to the outer exit. She stationed herself in front of the door, so that he couldn't open it. Mason gave her a quick glance and then turned and started back up the stairs. She ran after him.

"Okay. So you don't care about me. Think about Momma. Do you want them to call her in and yell at her? Please, Mason. It's not for me. It's for Momma. She loves you. You want to make her feel bad? Do you?"

The stairwell was empty. Everyone else had escaped for home. It wasn't fair. Here she was, plodding all the way back up the dirty old staircase behind a five-year-old, begging him to do something that no one in his right mind would do—go face the AP.

Someone was coming around the turn of the landing, taking two steps at a time, the sound a hollow echo through the stairwell. And then, right in front of them was Lupe, leaping like a deer. She stopped just a few steps above them.

"Trouble, huh?" she said, jerking her head toward Mason.

Vinnie felt a little prick of jealousy. How had Lupe managed to stay behind with Mr. Clayton after school was out? "I got to take him to the office," Vinnie said. "Mason. You come here this minute. Mr. Sharp . . ."

"C'mon, man," Lupe said, bouncing upon a surprised Mason and taking his hand, turning him around before he knew which way was front. She started back down the stairs with him, leaving Vinnie standing openmouthed.

"I'll walk him home," Lupe said. "You go tell the AP to pick on someone his own size." She grinned. "Like me."

"But . . ."

"You can show me the way, can't you, big guy?"

To Vinnie's amazement, Mason nodded, readjusting his small hand so it nested comfortably into Lupe's long-fingered one.

Vinnie was letting her brother go off with someone she hardly knew, someone the AP thought of as a criminal, but what could she do? She'd be chasing Mason all through Gertrude B. Spitzer until nighttime. Vinnie followed them and waited on the landing of the main floor until their footsteps died out and she could hear below her the sound of the east door opening and closing. Then she turned and reluctantly headed back toward the center of the building.

Mrs. Paxton and the AP had disappeared into the main office and were now deep in conversation with Dr. Munchen. She could tell by the way they were talking and gesturing that the principal was arguing with the AP. Mrs. Paxton was doing a little dance around the outside trying to jam a word in edgewise.

Vinnie stood there for a while before anyone even noticed her. It didn't help to eavesdrop. They were speaking that high-flown, antiseptic school language that only teachers and principals could understand. The words, that is. The feelings were clear. Mason was a menace and so, probably, was she.

"What's the matter, Vinnie?" It was the kind, sweet

voice of Mr. Clayton. Someday my prince will come—and there he was. Just when she needed him the most. She wished she could throw her arms around him.

"My brother," she managed to squeak out.

The principal, the AP, Mrs. Paxton—they all stopped chattering and gesturing and stared at her.

"Where *is* your brother, young lady? Didn't I tell you to bring him back?"

"He's gone." She didn't look at the AP when she spoke.

"What do you mean, gone?" The AP stood so close over her that she could see little bristly hairs growing out of his nostrils. Some of them were white. "What do you mean, gone?" he said again, louder than before.

"He—he left. He—he got away from me. He's very fast when he wants to be."

"Go after him!" Mrs. Paxton cried, suddenly turning back into a kindergarten teacher who cared about her children.

"Come on," Mr. Clayton said. "I'll go with you. We'll catch up to him." He started walking fast out of the office and down toward the east door. It was just like the handsome prince riding up on his great white horse, coming to the rescue when it seemed that all was lost. Vinnie skipped, danced, ran after him down the dingy corridor.

Outside on the walk, Mr. Clayton stopped. "My car's just at the corner of the playground . . ." He hesitated. "To heck with it. This is an emergency, right?"

To ride in Mr. Clayton's car! Just with him. And what a car it was—low and sleek, shiny bright, absolutely clean and waxed, and red, red as her new plastic barrettes.

"It's beautiful," she whispered as he unlocked the door and opened it for her.

He ran around to the other side. "Now. Which way would he have gone?"

It was her turn to hesitate. If she sent him the usual

61

way, they would catch up with Lupe and Mason in no time. "Turn around and go down the next right," she said. She'd take him the long way.

"Is he liable to do anything crazy?" Mr. Clayton's big freckled hand was on the gearshift almost touching her knee.

"Crazy?" Everything Mason did was crazy.

"Run out in front of a car? Run away? You know—anything dangerous?"

"He knows the rules," she said. "He'll be okay, I think." She didn't want Mr. Clayton worrying too much about Mason. Besides Lupe could make him behave. She'd seen that. Vinnie touched a hair clip and stroked her hair. Did he think she was pretty at all?

"Now explain to me. What offense was your brother hauled down to headquarters for?" He made Mason's trip to the office sound like a detective story.

"He spit in everybody's juice."

"That would make how many cups?"

"Twenty they said."

"Twenty. Who would have thought the young lad had so much spit in him!" He laughed. "I'm quoting Shakespeare, sort of."

Vinnie giggled. She couldn't help it. She wasn't sure who Shakespeare was, but Mr. Clayton made Mason sound almost neat. "Nobody likes him 'cause he won't talk."

"Won't or can't?"

"Won't. He used to talk fine."

Mr. Clayton slowed at the corner. She pointed him straight ahead. He shifted gears again. He was so hand-some from the side. His ear stuck out from his head just a little bit. It made him seem even cuter somehow. "Turn right at the next corner," she said. She hated to cut short the trip, but she didn't want him getting suspicious.

She had made the ride last as long as she could. She was afraid as they rounded the last corner that there they'd be—Lupe and Mason—coming from the other direction. How could she explain that? But luckily, there was no one in sight.

"This is my house," she said. If only there were grass in the yard. "I'd better run in and see if he's home yet."

She jumped out, leaving the car door open in her haste. She poked her head in the door, pretended to yell something, and then ran back to the car. "He's here," she said, "safe and sound. Thanks for the ride." She pushed the door shut. "Better turn around in the driveway." She didn't want him meeting Mason and Lupe on his way to the school.

He backed up the car, giving her a wave as he turned. She watched the car disappear around the curve and then began to run in the opposite direction down the block. She was out of breath before she reached the corner, where she could see Lupe and Mason ambling down the street. She held her aching side and watched them come.

Lupe was still holding Mason's hand. Every now and then she bent toward him and said something—like a stork over a baby chick. If you didn't know better, you'd think they were having a perfectly normal conversation. Lupe didn't look like the relative of a murderer—like the daughter. Maybe she was telling the truth. Maybe her father didn't do it.

When they got up to where Vinnie stood waiting, Lupe dropped Mason's hand and gave him a little pat on the rear. "Here you go," she said. She didn't act surprised that Vinnie was there ahead of them. "See you," she said to Mason. Mason smiled back—a perfectly normal little-kid smile. "Gotta go to work," she said.

"In the pumpkin patch?" It sounded mean. Vinnie hadn't really meant it to be.

63

"Nah. I cut pumpkins in the morning before school. I work"—she waved her hand backward—"for Mrs. Winston afternoons." That would explain the big house and yard.

Vinnie meant to thank her, at least to be polite. But before she got the words figured out, Lupe had turned away and was jogging down the street, her flip-flops slapping her heels. It was nearly November. Was she going to wear those stupid things all winter?

She turned angrily to Mason. "Boy, are you in trouble," she said. And then she remembered that lovely car, that wonderful ride. How could she be too mad at Mason? She'd just had a ride all by herself in Mr. Clayton's practically brand-new red sports car. Totally against the rules. A ride that would be hard to explain—to anyone.

"I'm not telling Momma *this* time," she said, taking the hand Lupe had held, "but I can't promise you Mr. Sharp won't." Mason shook her hand loose and started down the street alone, his little back straight and proud. "He was really mad!" she yelled, but Mason pretended not to hear.

7

Now that Vinnie knew where Mr. Clayton parked his car, she took the long way round to school so that she could go past it. She ran her finger lightly across the bright red fender, then took out a tissue and rubbed the spot. She wouldn't want to leave a stray smudged fingerprint on the gleaming surface.

It didn't seem odd to her that a man like Mr. Clayton should have such a showy car. It was exciting—as if he had a secret side that only she, Vinnie, knew about.

None of the other kids had ridden in the car. She felt sure of that. The way Mr. Clayton acted yesterday, it had to be against the law for teachers to give rides to kids. Her heart fluttered in a little thrill of delight. He had broken the law for her.

The first bell sounded. Reluctantly, she left the car and hurried toward the school. Part of her wanted everyone to know about her ride with Mr. Clayton and the other part was glad that she couldn't tell them. It was a secret between her and Mr. Clayton. She touched one of her barrettes. Two secrets now.

Mr. Clayton was standing at the classroom door as the children came in. "Your brother—everything okay?" he asked her.

"Yessir, thank you." She couldn't, of course, mention the car or the ride, but she tried to put a little extra feeling into the "thank you" so he'd understand that she meant thanks for the ride as well as thanks for asking about Mason.

At recess time she lagged a bit, straightening her books, picking up some trash from the floor.

"Nice and warm today," he said. "Better get out and enjoy it." She tried not to think that he was rushing her away.

She hated recess. What was she supposed to do with herself? She looked about, half afraid to see Lupe coming toward her, but Lupe was nowhere in sight. Where was she? Should Vinnie thank her for helping with Mason? She didn't want to thank Lupe. She was annoyed with Lupe. Why had Lupe tried to make her think that was *her* house and yard when she was only raking leaves for money? And what was Vinnie supposed to believe about Lupe's father? Was he a murderer or wasn't he? Maybe Lupe was trying to trick her into thinking her dad was innocent when all along . . . Vinnie felt all sweaty just thinking about murder and jail and a friend who turned out not to be one—a flip-flop friend, wasn't that what Lupe had called the man?

A little knot of girls led by Heather was heading in her direction. Maybe—maybe they'd decided to be nice after all. Mr. Clayton was always telling the class they had to be a team. Maybe—

"We heard your little brother is the worst kid in kindergarten," a girl named Taylor said.

"He has psychological problems, doesn't he?" Heather was so smart. It made Vinnie sick. She looked at her. Was this supposed to be a trick question?

"It's okay," Heather continued in a smarmy grown-up voice. "My mother's best friend is the room mother for Mrs. Paxton's afternoon session. Mrs. Paxton talks over all her *problems* with her." She said the word "problems" in a way that made Vinnie want to sock her in the teeth. Mason's "problems" were none of Heather Carson's dumb mother's best friend's business.

"*My* mother thinks it's because he's still upset about his father's death." Did Heather think she was the school psychologist or something? "Vinnie's father died just before she moved here," she said. Now she was talking as though Vinnie weren't standing right there. The other girls murmured something that was supposed to sound like they were sorry for poor Vinnie, but it was so fake—as though they were all better than Vinnie because their fathers hadn't up and died on them.

"Children are known to misbehave when a parent dies. My mother—"

"Your mother doesn't know piddledy. It's none of her blinking business."

The whole group gasped and drew back as though Vinnie had threatened them.

"You don't have to be angry," Heather said, a slight note of disapproval creeping into her smooth grown-up voice. "My mother—"

"Will you just shut up about your stupid mother! She doesn't know anything!"

Heather's eyebrows went up. "You can say whatever you want to about me, but I'll thank you not to insult—"

"Come on. Come on." It was Lupe, breaking through the prissy knot of Heather's gang. She took Vinnie's arm and pushed her back through the circle. "Leave her alone."

"We were just trying to be sympathetic," Heather said. "Her brother—"

"Her brother is just fine."

"My brother is none of anybody's business." Vinnie shook Lupe's hand off her arm and went over to the corner of the building, pretending to watch the boys trying to get balls in the basket. They hadn't improved.

Lupe followed her and leaned against the building beside her as though they were friends or something.

Just then Vinnie noticed Lupe's feet. She wasn't wearing flip-flops. She was wearing gigantic black high-top sneakers. There was no sign of socks, but she did have on genuine sneakers.

"You got sneakers." It popped out. She hadn't planned to say anything.

Lupe sniffed with embarrassed pleasure. "Clayton gave them to me," she said. "They used to be his." She drew a circle on the pavement with her toe. "I got to wear them. Might hurt his feelings." You could tell she was as proud as could be. "Besides," she added with a funny grin, "they're just like some my pop used to have."

Vinnie's hand went to a barrette, then fell. Still, she was the only one to have had a ride in his car. Wasn't that better than sneakers?

That night in bed, she thought about the sneakers— they really bugged her. But why should she mind? Lupe only had flip-flops. Well, no one knew that for sure. All anybody knew was that she would only *wear* flip-flops. Anybody who wanted sneakers could buy them. At the discount store you could get them for less than five dollars—not brand name—but sneakers. Better than flip-flops. Five dollars was less than the price of one big pumpkin. Lupe could have bought sneakers if she'd wanted them. Or at the Salvation Army. Ask Grandma, she was the queen of Salvation Army bargains. Lupe was probably just trying to get sympathy with those flip-flops—get Mr. Clayton's attention.

Mr. Clayton felt sorry for Lupe—people thinking her father was a murderer and all. Vinnie felt sorry for her, too. She lived in that terrible pumpkin shack. She had a peculiar name and weird clothes. The girl was strange herself. Sure, she felt sorry for her but that didn't mean that Vinnie wanted Lupe to think she was going to be her friend. Nobody would ever like Vinnie if Lupe kept barging in. And being Mason's sister put Vinnie in enough trouble with Mr. Sharp as it was. If he thought she hung around Lupe Mahoney . . .

It was good nobody knew that Lupe took Mason home yesterday. They'd think for sure that she was in thick with Vinnie's family.

Why did Mason just take Lupe's hand and walk home with her? Why wasn't he scared? Lupe was the weirdest person in Gertrude B. Spitzer School. Takes one to know one, Grandma says. Grandma ought to know weird.

Vinnie remembered liking Grandma when she was small—when Daddy was alive. She would come once a year and spend Christmas with them in the apartment. She always brought presents, though not the presents Vinnie would have chosen—underpants that were too small or cheap books from the supermarket with baby stories. But Vinnie hadn't minded. Grandma would read the stories aloud and make all the voices. Mason would shriek with laughter and even Vinnie would have to giggle. Grandma looked so funny pursing her lips.

"'Peep. Peep. Peep, cried Baby Bird while Mr. Cat licked his chops.'"

Vinnie didn't know at first what "chops" were. She only knew pork chops. But Grandma stopped reading and rolled her eyes and stuck her tongue way out, licking beyond her bright red lips with their little red-lined wrinkles to show what Mr. Cat was doing.

Vinnie tried to remember when she'd stopped liking Grandma. It was after Daddy got sick the last time. What had Grandma done? She was always trying to be too helpful, but not with Daddy—she hardly ever went into Daddy's room even though Daddy was her own stepson. No, she was always messing around in the kitchen or making Vinnie and Mason do something, so that Momma had to be extra patient with her as well as take care of Daddy and everything else.

There was the day Grandma took Vinnie and Mason to the movies. It wasn't even a movie Vinnie wanted to see. Vinnie tried to say no, but Grandma sort of pushed her out of the apartment. This was a crazy cartoon movie where the characters beat one another up or chased one another off cliffs. The worse it got, the more Mason laughed and cheered and the colder Vinnie's stomach felt.

Something was wrong at home. Terribly wrong. She started out of her seat. "I want to go home," she said.

Her grandmother shoved her back down. "Shh," she said. "Not now. See, Mason loves it. Wait 'til after the show."

But after the show Grandma made them go window-shopping and afterward stop for ice cream. Then they took a long ride underground on the Metro and then, just when she thought they might be going home at last, Grandma decided they should transfer to a bus and ride around topside for a while.

They didn't get home until way after dark. When they did, Daddy's bed was empty. He was dead. Dead and gone. Grandma had taken her away, and while she was gone Daddy had died. If she'd been there . . . In some part of her mind she knew that there was nothing she could have done to save him, and yet—yet she should have been there to try.

It was probably her daddy calling out to her that had made her want to leave the movie and go home. Vinnie had heard about things like that—people in terrible situations calling to their loved ones far away and their loved ones hearing them. But Grandma wouldn't let her go home.

At the time she'd only thought about herself—how she hadn't been there when Daddy needed her. Now, for the first time, she wondered about Grandma. Grandma must have known that Daddy was about to die. Why had *she* left him? She was his mother. Well, stepmother, but the only mother Daddy had. Mothers were supposed to be there when their children needed them. What was the matter with Grandma that she had made sure she wasn't there when Daddy died?

And the day after the funeral, the only time Vinnie could remember when Momma broke down and cried in front of everybody, Grandma just got all chirpy and fake cheerful and took Vinnie and Mason to the other room to watch TV. She'd never figure Grandma out, but she hadn't thought she'd have to. After all, Grandma wasn't around all that much. She'd never have imagined that someday Grandma would be in charge.

Grandma didn't act like a grown-up in charge. Momma was always so careful about what they ate and when, but Grandma thought it was great if Mason ate anything at all. She bought big boxes of sugared cereal and urged Mason to eat the junk all over the house any old time of day.

When Vinnie tried to tell her that too much sugar was not good for Mason, Grandma read the side of the cereal box out loud. But that's an *advertisement* Vinnie wanted to say—of course they'll tell you it's good for kids. But Vinnie didn't say anything. She felt too tired to fight. Momma was supposed to be the one to set the rules, not Vinnie. Momma should be telling Grandma what to feed them and what not. Vinnie was only nine years old. She shouldn't have to keep Grandma in line.

The money had run out. That was why they'd had to move to Grandma's house. That was why she'd had to leave Shawna Watts, her only true friend in the entire world, and move to some little ratty town in the south part of Virginia that no one in Washington, D.C., had ever heard of in their lives—why they'd had to leave Daddy up there in that cold cemetery far away.

*V*innie didn't even want to think about Christmas. Last year, they'd hardly noticed it. Daddy was in the middle of another round of chemotherapy and was sick all the time. Chemo was supposed to make him better. It did for a while, but then he died anyway. It was all a waste. She hated to remember last Christmas. They wouldn't even have had a Santa Claus if Grandma hadn't done it. Vinnie could tell Grandma had filled the stockings. Hers was stuffed with a used Barbie doll from the Salvation Army, a pair of hand-knit mittens, and all kinds of chocolate Christmas shapes that must have been on sale from other Christmases. They tasted like stale wax.

She lied to Shawna. From TV commercials, she made up all this good stuff that she'd gotten. When Shawna wanted to come play with her great things, she had to say that since they were so upset about her daddy being so sick from the treatments, they couldn't have any company. Which was almost true. Anyhow, after a while Shawna forgot or maybe she didn't believe Vinnie in the first place.

Now it was almost Christmas again. Vinnie caught snatches of conversation from the other kids about what they were getting, but there was no need for her to lie this year. No one asked her.

For once she was glad to be on the outside. What could she have said? She certainly wasn't going to get a computer or a stereo or even a computer game or some CDs. Grandma didn't have anything to play games or CDs on. Vinnie couldn't even have the fun of pretending about Santa Claus for Mason. How could you ask a five-year-old who wouldn't talk what he wanted Santa to bring him? And if, by some miracle, he'd tell you, you knew he'd just be disappointed. It wouldn't be fair to get a kid all excited when he'd be lucky to get two pairs of new socks and a pack of bubble gum.

She understood all this so well, how could she have made such a dumb mistake? How could she have wondered out loud what to give Mr. Clayton for Christmas? Her mother sighed, having forgotten that in small towns all the kids gave the teacher a present. But Grandma brightened right up. "Teachers in this town love homemade things," she said. "I'll whip you up something scrumptious."

"No!" said Vinnie. She knew Grandma's scrumptious. Her cookies were so hard you were liable to crack a tooth. "Mr. Clayton," she lied, "is like a health-food nut. He doesn't touch sweets."

"Well, I could make him a scarf then, or mittens."

"Mr. Clayton—"

Her mother tried to help. "That's thoughtful, Mother, but yarn is so expensive, I hate—"

"No problem, as they say." And before anyone could

think up a way to stop her, Grandma was unraveling a hideous fuchsia sweater, rolling the fake wool into a giant ball, and knitting it into a scarf about a foot wide.

"Here," she said, holding out the knitting to Vinnie. "This is duck soup. I'll show you how, and you can do the rest. It'll mean more to the teacher if he knows you made the gift yourself."

Vinnie shrank back as though someone were trying to hand her a rattlesnake. The idea of giving Mr. Clayton a scarf in that hideous color of used yarn was horrible enough. But for him to think for one minute that she, Vinnie, had chosen the yarn—had made the scarf . . .

"Go on, Vinnie. Knitting's fun." She couldn't believe it, her mother was urging her to do it. Couldn't Momma understand that Vinnie would rather have chicken pox in her throat than give a present like that to Mr. Clayton?

Grandma could not take a hint. When Vinnie refused to work on the scarf, she made it herself. She finished the wretched thing the night before the last day of school, then wrapped the scarf in used wrapping paper she'd found in the attic and tied it with a pieced-together length of paper ribbon. "Here," she said proudly, giving the package to Vinnie the next morning, "he'll love it. Guaranteed."

At the edge of the playground was a trash barrel. Vinnie glimpsed around to make sure no one was watching, then dropped the parcel in. Better no gift at all than one that the other kids would sneer at—or worse, one that would make Mr. Clayton have to try too hard to be nice about.

Everyone except Vinnie was in a holiday mood. Presents were piled high on Mr. Clayton's desk. Vinnie slunk to her seat, her eyes on her desktop. Maybe no one would notice that she hadn't brought anything to the teacher.

She could have brought a poem. Why hadn't she thought of it? He'd love that, and no one else would do such a thing. It'd be homemade, like Grandma said. She bit the tip of her hair. Stupid! She'd been so determined *not* to give him Grandma's scarf that she hadn't even thought about what she *could* bring. And now it was too late.

Well, maybe not. She tore loose a piece of notebook paper. Maybe there was still time. Think. She smoothed out the ragged holes with her finger. No. She shouldn't have ripped the paper out. It looked so careless and messy. She balled it up and stuck it under the seat. Then she opened the notebook rings and carefully took out a fresh sheet. She just had to think. She bit her hair, then her pencil. "Christmas," she wrote down neatly on the top line. The capital *C* looked wobbly. She erased it. "Christmas," she wrote again.

Out of the corner of her eye she saw that Lupe had stopped by the teacher's desk and slid something into the pile. Even the flip-flop girl who lived in a pumpkin shack and whose daddy was in jail had brought the teacher a present.

She erased "Christmas" and wrote "A Gift." No, that sounded prissy. She erased again.

The bell rang, and all she had on her paper was a hole from erasing too much. She started to ball up the paper, but stopped. She'd write her poem out on this sheet, then when she got it right, she'd copy it onto a fresh piece of paper. That's the way real poets did it. They didn't start with a new piece of paper all the time. They did rough drafts. Mr. Clayton was always telling them how real writers worked. He probably knew a lot of writers personally.

She took her pencil and paper to the playground at recess time. Stupid again. She should have brought something to press on. She looked around for a smooth place to write, but, of course, there was no place on a playground you could use as a desk. Even the flat surfaces were bumpy or splintery. Besides, her teeth were chattering, and since she hadn't put on her mittens, her fingers were so frozen she had trouble holding the pencil. Maybe she could go into the girls' room. It was quiet there—

"Excuse me, Vinnie." She had nearly bumped into Mr. Clayton, who was coming out the back door.

"No, excuse me, sir. I—" Vinnie started in disbelief. Mr. Clayton was wearing a tan windbreaker, a plaid cap, and Grandma's fuchsia scarf.

He was grinning like a proud parent. "Like it?" He patted the scarf. "Unique color, huh?" There wasn't a trace of mockery in his voice. "She must have made it for me herself." He fingered the yarn, looking over Vinnie's head across the playground. "There she is. Excuse me." He stepped around Vinnie and headed toward the old jungle gym, where Lupe was leaning, watching the boys bounce the ball off the side of the hoop.

Vinnie opened her mouth, but shut it again. Lupe? How could she tell him that Lupe had no more made that scarf than a pollywog? How could she explain that Lupe had taken the scarf out of the trash barrel? How could she say "It's really *my* present. I might have even made it myself. I almost did. If I had thought for one minute you might like it, I would have"?

Mr. Clayton was talking to Lupe now. She was smiling shyly and drawing circles with her sneaker toe on the pavement. *His* sneaker toe. He had given her those lousy sneakers, and because she had feet like a gigantic duck she could wear them. Whoever heard of a ten- or eleven-year-old girl with feet as big as a man's?

Her fury carried her through lunch and the whole of

the afternoon. Mr. Clayton had taken off the scarf, but not his braggy parent face. She caught him grinning at Lupe at least three times. Well, she couldn't care less about the stupid scarf or the stupid sneakers. I'll write a poem, the best poem I've ever written—the best poem Mr. Clayton has ever seen and I'll mail it to him or take it to his house. I'll find out where he lives and take it to him. Somehow.

"Class," he'll say, "I want to share with you the best poem I have ever read." Then he'll turn around and smile at me. "I've never taught such a gifted student. Such color! Such feeling! Listen . . ."

But her brain stopped there. It wouldn't give her the poem itself—not even the first line of a poem. Not even a decent title.

She sat in her desk chewing her hair and watching him, trying to squeeze something out of her tight, dry head, when it dawned on her that Jenny Painter in the seat behind her was yelling. She looked around. Everyone was yelling—no, cheering—and Mr. Clayton was standing up front with a funny red face that shone through his hair, smiling an embarrassed smile. What were they all cheering about? What? She hadn't been listening. Who could she ask?

The bell rang and everyone jumped up to go—the holidays at last. Several people stopped to speak to Mr. Clayton. He blushed each time.

As she walked toward the door she watched him, trying to get some clue. "You going?" It was Lupe. Vinnie wanted to ignore her. Hadn't she stolen Vinnie's present and then lied and said she'd made it herself? She wanted to snub Lupe, but she had to ask someone what was going on.

"Where? What do you mean?"

"You know. Clayton's wedding." Vinnie looked at her. She felt as though someone had smacked her in the face. "He invited us," Lupe went on. "All of us. He just said, 'I want all of you to come.'"

"You're lying!" She had to be lying. Vinnie started to push her way through the crowd at the door.

"Merry Christmas!" Mr. Clayton called out, but he didn't mean her. He was nice to everybody—to anybody. He didn't really care.

She was out the east door before she remembered Mason. Stupid Mason. She fought back her tears and went in again to get him. At the street corner she grabbed his hand. He snatched it away, and so Vinnie, sobbing and yelling, had to chase him all the way home.

Christmas. How could she care about Christmas? Momma tried. She bought Vinnie a pair of the same brand sneakers that Heather and Taylor wore, leather ones with the name in red letters on the side. Vinnie didn't know how Momma knew what the regular kids were wearing, yet somehow Momma had found out and spent the money to get Vinnie a pair. Vinnie tried hard to be grateful. But before she had a chance to wear them even once, Mason took them and scribbled all over them with a purple Magic Marker.

"Oh, Mason," Momma cried out, "what will I do with you?" First Momma, then Grandma scrubbed the sneakers with soapy water and bleach, but the faint purple splotch remained like the pink blot on the playground. *Congratulations, Mr. C.*

Momma said she was proud of Vinnie for not making a scene. She didn't know that in Vinnie's mind having her beautiful new sneakers messed up was something that was bound to happen. Nothing ever turned out right for

79

her. Daddy was dead. Shawna Watts was far away in Washington. And somewhere in this awful town Mr. Clayton was getting married.

Vinnie watched so much TV over the holidays, even Grandma got worried. "I don't have anything to do," Vinnie said. What she meant was she didn't have anything to do that would keep her mind captive, keep it from straying into pain-filled thought, into aching memory.

9

She didn't want to go to school. She couldn't go. Something had happened to her teeth. It was as though tiny people with metal files had snuck up on her while she was asleep and filed all her teeth into sharp points. When Momma put her head in the door to call her, she pretended to be dead asleep. She was positive that Momma would not accept sharp teeth as an excuse for absence.

"Please, Vinnie, get up and get going. This is the day I have to take Mason to Charlottesville, and I don't have time to fool around."

Vinnie squinched her eyes even tighter together. They hadn't had money to buy Mr. Clayton a proper present. They hadn't had money for a turkey dinner for themselves, but somehow, magically, there was enough to drag precious Mason to still another fancy specialist more than an hour away, who would end up saying what all the others had: "The boy is deeply disturbed over his father's death. It will take time and patience and lots of love. Two hundred dollars, please."

"Vinnie!"

There. She knew it. Her sharp teeth had bitten the side of her mouth. It would probably start bleeding. How could she go to school with a bloody mouth? How? She sighed. Sometime over the holidays, Mr. Clayton had gotten married. She didn't know when or where, she hadn't been listening. But who would want to go to his stupid wedding anyway?

Well at least it showed Lupe what was what. He hadn't liked *her* best either. He'd gone off and married somebody none of them had ever heard of. Vinnie had no proof of this. It wasn't a huge city, just a smallish town. Somebody in the class might know the woman, but she doubted it. He probably wanted to fool them all, make them think that his "team" was his whole life, and all the time he had this secret life that he never even hinted to them about.

And what about that car? It wasn't a married man's car. It was the car of somebody a little bit wild and free. Married people had to be careful and pinch their pennies. They didn't go out and blow all their money on a bright red sports car. He probably never meant to get married. He probably got trapped by some flashy woman who just wanted his car. The marriage wouldn't last. It probably wouldn't last out the month.

"Vinnie, I mean it! Get moving."

She dragged herself out of bed and padded downstairs. She could smell the scorched oatmeal immediately. Grandma was making breakfast. Vinnie stood just inside the kitchen door. The linoleum froze her bare feet.

"Hey, pretty girl, get yourself some clothes on!" Grandma was trying to scrape the burned oatmeal off the bottom of the pot. Momma was at the table trying to coax Mason into opening his mouth so she could poke in a spoonful of oatmeal. Mason's mouth was clamped down tighter than a clamshell. You couldn't even see his lips.

"Just one bite, sweetie. Come on. Just a bite." Momma looked up at Vinnie. "You heard your grandmother," she said.

"I don't feel so good." Stomachaches were more believable excuses than sharp teeth. Besides, she was really beginning to get one.

Grandma came over and ran her hand up and down Vinnie's bare arm. "Feels good to me," she said, laughing, as usual, at her own dumb joke.

"Come here, Vinnie." Her mother put down the spoon and felt Vinnie's forehead with her cool hand. "I think you're all right," she said. "Just a little too much Christmas." Too much Christmas! Where had she been when everyone was having all this Christmas? Momma had given her a pair of sneakers that Mason had already ruined. That was *her* Christmas. "Just get some warm clothes on. Fast! It's much too cold to run around barefoot in your nightie."

"My stomach hurts." It was hardly a lie anymore. Her stomach was feeling worse by the minute—sort of a dull pain with a little sharp point in the middle.

"Well, of course it hurts," Grandma chimed in. "It's empty. You run and dress before your nice oatmeal gets all cold. It'll put starch in your pinafore! Turn you into a new woman. Guaranteed."

Vinnie looked at Momma, begging silently for support, but Momma had already gone back to Mason as though she believed oatmeal might just turn *him* into a new person. Lots o' luck.

She'd show Momma. Instead of the sneakers Momma

had bought, she put on Grandma's Salvation Army clothes—short dress, brown shoes, and all. That would pay Momma back. When Vinnie came into the kitchen, Momma glanced quickly at her feet. "Mason ruined the sneakers," Vinnie said, "like he does everything."

Momma's mouth went into a tight line. "All right, big boy," she said, "open up," as though Vinnie were a rude stranger she'd chosen to ignore.

Meantime, Grandma's oatmeal had turned to stone. Burned stone. Vinnie pushed the bowl away. "I told you I didn't feel good. You make me eat this stuff I'll vomit."

"Vinnie!" Now she had Momma's full attention. Her voice was low, but she carved every word out clear as ice. "You sit there and eat that oatmeal. I do not want to hear another word out of you and I do not want to see one bite left in that bowl. Then you get up and get yourself to school. And if you *ever* speak to your grandmother like that again . . ." She left the threat hanging in the air.

The kitchen clock ticked loudly. The refrigerator hummed into life. No one moved. Not even Mason, who sat still so long with his mouth open that Momma finally saw it and slipped in two spoonfuls of oatmeal before he noticed.

She would be late for school. There was no helping it. Why couldn't she just be absent? This one day. It wouldn't hurt anything. She was going to throw up if she had to eat this stuff. Momma was watching her. She put a spoonful into her mouth and sloshed it down with a big gulp of milk. If I take a long time . . .

Momma gave up on Mason and went to get their coats. But she didn't do as Vinnie hoped. She didn't leave. Instead, she stood over Vinnie until every blinking spoonful of oatmeal had been put in the front of Vinnie's mouth and washed down with a huge swallow of milk. It took two full glasses. Every gulp made Vinnie sure she was going to vomit. Even with all the milk, the oatmeal stopped like a rock in her throat. But when she gave the least hint of gagging, her mother's eyebrow went up and dared her, just dared her to throw up.

The streets were empty. At first she ran, getting all sweaty under her winter jacket. She *would* throw up if she kept running. Besides, what was the rush? She was already tardy. You didn't get points for being just a *little* tardy instead of a lot tardy. Tardy was tardy, right? And Momma had been so mad at her for dawdling she wouldn't give her a note. Vinnie slowed down to a Mason crawl.

Just at the picket fence there was a fallen branch on the sidewalk. She stripped off the leaves and ran it across the fence palings as she walked. She loved to scrape sticks across these palings—especially this morning. It made such a wonderful angry rattle. If she had a rattlesnake, where would she put it right now? In Momma's car so it would bite Mason? She recoiled from the thought. What if it struck Momma instead? As mad as she was at Momma, she didn't want Momma to die. She'd be an orphan then. Living with Mason and Grandma. Eating scorched oatmeal every morning of her life. She'd rather die.

Her stomach went cold. No, she didn't want to die. Although everyone would really be sorry if she did. Even Mason would be sorry. He'd probably end up so crazy mixed-up they'd have to put him in a mental institution for the rest of his life.

There was a corner of her mind that smiled at the thought of Mason locked away for life, but she didn't like the idea enough to die for it.

And what about Mr. Clayton? Would he care if she

died? Would he even notice? He never even told her he was getting married—just the whole dumb, snotty class, and he made sure he picked a time when she wasn't listening. He knew when kids weren't listening all right. He always knew. Even when he had his back to the class and was writing a problem on the board. He'd call out someone's name to work the problem, and that person would be the only one in the whole class who wasn't paying attention. He did it every time. He was famous for it.

It was mean of him to pick on her. He should have known how shocked she'd be. She'd just been riding in his car a few days before. He'd given her barrettes and made her think she was someone special—different from all the others—the only one who wrote poetry. He was a—a flip-flop man. He made her think she was so great and then flipped right around and made Lupe think he liked her the best, when really he liked someone neither Vinnie nor Lupe had ever heard of the best of all—liked her so much that he went and married her without any warning.

There it was—his stupid, show-off red car parked on the side street by the corner of the playground, like always. As though nothing had changed. When everything—*everything*—had changed. He'd made her believe she could count on him and then he'd gone and left her—just like Daddy. She walked past the car. She twisted her neck around to look at it again.

Red was an angry color, a furious color. She went back to where the red car sat—fat and smug. Red was Mason's favorite color in all the world. All at once Vinnie hated red—red Life Savers, red barrettes, red cars . . .

She took a barrette out of her hair and, with the sharp point of the metal prong, she slowly and deliberately drew a line straight across the shiny red fender. Her stomach was no longer cold and nauseated. She dug a second line, a third, another, until she was scratching, scratching—back and forth—gouges so deep the silver bled from underneath. Her whole body glowed. There was a terrible screech in her ears—worse than long fingernails on a blackboard. The barrette shrieked across the gleaming finish—up and down, side to side—a long screaming silver line from the fender to the handle of the door. She was panting hard, but she didn't mind. She had never felt so strong—so powerful—so drunk with fury. *Screech, screech, screech.* What a hideous, wicked, evil, wonderful sound. *Screech, screech, screech.*

Suddenly she saw them, in the center of the passenger door—the very door he'd opened for her. Two sickening gray initials etched deeply into the red—LM—her initials.

She tried to brush them away with the heel of her palm. Someone would see them. Mr. Clayton would know. She looked about. Had anyone been watching? Chilly tentacles of fear wriggled into the heat of her fury. She was no longer warm, no longer panting. She was hardly breathing at all. A cold terror squeezed her stomach. She backed away from the car—the ruined fender, the scarred door. She backed across the sidewalk, into the school fence, then, avoiding the car as though it were about to explode, she walked around it and out into the street. Something hurt. The barrette. It was cutting into the flesh of her palm. She flung it high into the air. It cleared the tall fence and plinked on the concrete near the rusting jungle gym.

The windows of the school building looked down at her like rows of staring eyes. She began to run. The sweat was pouring out of her hair. The neck of her jacket seemed to choke her as she ran, her back to those gaping eyes, to the grim playground, to the terrible scar on the bright red door.

10

She had never known what the TV ads meant when they talked about "offensive body odor." But when you're hiding in the laundry basket, you learn fast. Face it—she lived in a smelly family. The smells were vaguely familiar; sorted out, they wouldn't seem so bad—except maybe Mason's—but piled together in an enormous clothes hamper the stink was overpowering.

Momma—she'd always loved the way Momma smelled, ever since she was tiny and nestled against Momma to be read to. Sometimes she would think how good Momma smelled—like flowers in the park in spring. Sometimes she just smelled her and forgot to listen to the story. But even Momma's smell turned wrong—like eating too many jelly doughnuts at one time. Besides, her smell was now mixed up with Grandma and Mason. Vinnie never wanted to smell them. When Mason was a baby, powdered and freshly diapered right after a bath, he'd smelled nice then. But not anymore. And Grandma. What did she wear that she thought smelled nice? Even in the open air, the sharp sweetness of her smell made your eyes want to water. Vinnie couldn't sort out her own smell in the hamper. Maybe she didn't really know what she smelled like.

When she first got home—creeping up to the door— she heard Grandma's voice from the back of the house talking very loudly. Most of Grandma's friends were hard of hearing, so she always yelled into the telephone. Even when she was speaking regularly her voice was loud, but when she got on the phone it was like one of those drills they used in Washington to rip up the street.

Vinnie opened the door and sneaked up the stairs. So far so good. But where to hide? Grandma was sure to come barging right into Vinnie and Mason's bedroom. She was not big on observing other people's privacy— especially people who were smaller than she was.

The solution was right there in the upstairs hall staring her in the face. The laundry hamper—a huge woven basket with a hinged lid. She could climb in and pull the top down. And since it was woven, she wouldn't have to worry about breathing. She was so relieved that she almost forgot about her crime, her fear, her desperation. She also had forgotten about the laundry.

The basket was hardly half full, so the problem wasn't that there was no room inside. The problem was having to crouch there with her nose right above the laundry. It hadn't occurred to her that the fumes from her own family's dirty clothes would be poisonous. She'd heard of people dying from fumes—noxious fumes. The words popped into her head. She liked the sound of them. They sounded poisonous. Noxious. How do you suppose it was spelled? They'd need to use the word in the newspaper when they found her dead there.

She felt a tingle—not from fear of death, but a tingle of regret. "Death by noxious fumes" seemed almost romantic. Her regret was for Momma. Imagine the reporters swarming over the house, asking questions like:

"How does it *feel,* Mrs. Matthews, to know your daughter was suffocated by the noxious fumes from her own family's dirty laundry?"

Momma would hate that. She would be humiliated. When Daddy got sick and they got poorer and poorer, Momma still made sure they were clean. She was almost fanatic about it, changing Daddy's sheets and Mason's clothes two or three times a day. Which is why, even with Daddy gone, there was always laundry, no matter how often they washed.

Poor Momma. Vinnie sighed. Better, though, that Momma be embarrassed by noxious fumes killing her only daughter than by seeing her child sent to jail for vandalism. "Malicious destruction of private property"— she'd seen that phrase in the paper once. They'd sent the boys who'd done it to jail, too. In Washington vandals were always boys. A girl would seem worse.

Being in a small town didn't help. The town, as the AP had reminded them over the intercom, was "cracking down" on vandals. Cracking down—Vinnie imagined vandals with great, fat pieces of chalk writing on the side of a large, dark building that had cracked—right across the line of graffiti they had written—and tumbled down to crush the wrongdoers in a pile of stones and rubble.

She knew, of course, that all "cracking down" really meant was a policeman banging you on the head with one of those little baseball bats they carried. The whack would hurt like fury, but it probably wouldn't kill you.

You didn't get the electric chair for vandalism, she was sure of that. You got a bump on the head or jail, or, if the judge was kind, reform school. How many years did you get for malicious destruction of a car? A new, expensive car that was someone's pride and joy?

Jail would be terrible. She'd probably be the only child in it. Maybe Brownsville had juvenile detention like they had in Washington. Nobody had ever mentioned it. Not even Mr. Sharp. In the city almost everyone knew someone who'd been there. In a way, it might be better to go to a regular jail. The grown-ups, even if they were all criminals, would probably feel sorry for her—just a kid, a little girl, small for her age—being put in a jail.

How long had she been in the basket? Grandma's cuckoo clock would tell her the hours, but it hadn't sounded. At least she hadn't heard it. She had been too busy thinking. Vinnie always did that. Just when she most needed to listen, she'd go off into what Daddy used to call her "blue fuzz." She had to listen. The fumes were already affecting her brain. She could tell.

She crouched, curled up into herself like one of those unborn babies in the sex education book, holding her nose and breathing through her mouth. The house was almost silent. The furnace clicked on and whooshed hot air through the registers. She stopped breathing and strained to hear, leaning her ear against the side of the basket.

She could hear now the *thump thump* of her grandmother walking heavily on the kitchen linoleum. The thumping stopped. She listened for the clatter of dishes or the clang of pots, but there wasn't another sound. What could Grandma be doing?

Vinnie sighed and began to breathe through her nose again. She couldn't last much longer. If she didn't die first, Grandma would take Mason to school at twelve-thirty and then— Idiot, Mason wasn't here. Mason was in Charlottesville. He'd gone off to see his two billionth specialist. Momma would drop him off at school later. At three o'clock, he'd wait and wait at the kindergarten door for Vinnie to pick him up. When she didn't appear and they found out she was absent, they'd call Grandma—or Momma. Anyhow, Vinnie would probably not be able to get out of the hamper until late afternoon. She'd surely be dead by then. What a dumb place to hide. Stupid. Stupid. Stupid.

Wait. She stopped breathing again. She couldn't have imagined how noisy just breathing was. The heavy *thump, thump, thump* was going down the hall—coming up the stairs. Like in a ghost story. She froze, her eyes squinched shut like a baby who thinks if he can't see you, you can't see him.

"Well, mercy on us!" Light and air and her grandmother's amazed face appeared all at once above her. Vinnie's neck popped up like a turtle's as she strained to think of an excuse—some reason why she might be in the laundry basket. She crouched there blinking, banging about in her brain for a believable explanation—

"Don't you know you're supposed to take the clothes *off* before you throw them in here?"

The woman was trying to make a joke. It made Vinnie furious. Grandma should have been angry or even scared. She should have been demanding an explanation. It was hard to think up answers when you don't get the right question.

"C'mon," Grandma said. "Hop on out, so I can get the wash." She stuck out her hand, but Vinnie ignored it. She could at least climb out by herself, but she couldn't, not really. She tipped the basket over trying and had to crawl out like some worm from under a rock.

"Now let's get this washing." Vinnie helped pick up the clothes, the ones that had nearly cost her her life. They seemed so ordinary now—a T-shirt of Mason's, her own underpants, a slip of Grandma's, her mother's blue blouse. She threw them into Grandma's plastic laundry container. Grandma picked it up and started back down the stairs. Halfway down, she turned and looked up at Vinnie, who was standing dumbly in the upstairs hall like a laundry hamper herself.

"You going to school now?"

"I don't feel too good."

"Yeah, I know about that disease. Seems to run in the family. Your grandpa told me that your daddy suffered from that disease as a boy. Every Friday, regular. Terrible allergy to spelling tests. What's *your* complaint?"

She didn't know what to say. She couldn't claim spelling. She was a good speller—maybe the best in her class in Washington.

"C'mon down. Get yourself a glass of soda while I put this into the machine. Then I'll walk you over. Whatever it is, it won't improve putting it off."

No escape. She should have run away from home. Now it was too late. Vinnie changed her clothes. She took off her Salvation Army school dress and leather shoes and put on her jeans, a T-shirt, a blue cardigan, and her spoiled sneakers. The sweater had a tiny, round moth hole in it just beside the middle button, but it couldn't be helped. She smoothed back her hair. No barrettes now. She wouldn't think about that. She went downstairs and put on her jacket, waiting in the front hall for Grandma to finish fussing with the laundry.

"Don't you want a glass of soda or chocolate milk or something?" Grandma called from the kitchen.

Vinnie didn't answer. She certainly couldn't eat or drink anything. She would throw up for sure. She felt chilled and feverish already. As Grandma got her own coat, Vinnie forced open her frozen mouth enough to croak out, "I need a note." Her grandmother returned to the kitchen, scribbled something, and brought it back and handed it to her. Vinnie stuffed it into her jacket pocket without reading it. What did it matter? A tardy note wouldn't keep her out of jail.

All the way to school Grandma chattered away, as though it was perfectly normal for her to be walking Vinnie to school in the middle of the morning. She didn't even mention the fact that Vinnie had changed her clothes, though she must have noticed. The closer they got to school, the colder Vinnie became. She had seen a nature special once that told about people being frozen to death. They got sleepy, it said. The special must have been wrong. Vinnie wasn't the least bit sleepy. She was wide awake, so wide awake that her eyelids felt glued back. She was frozen and sweating at the same time. Her mouth and throat were so dry she couldn't have spit, much less spoken.

They got to the front steps of the building. Vinnie was sure Grandma would turn back then. She hated those steps, but the woman just kept going—puff—puff—her breath loud and scratchy—all the way up the long concrete stairs, into the door, and then down the hall, stopping once or twice to catch her breath. She huffed up the final two flights and on to the door of the classroom.

Don't leave me. Suddenly, Vinnie wanted her to stay. As crazy as that was, she didn't want Grandma to leave. But Grandma had already started to go. She'd stuck her head into the door and said in a whisper loud enough for all the class to hear, "She's a bit poorly today, but she does hate to miss." Then she gave Vinnie a little shove into the room and started back down the hall toward the stairs.

11

She walked to the cloakroom, hugging the wall, not looking at anybody. She half expected Mr. Clayton to call out to her, but he was busy at his desk. After she had hung up her jacket and empty book bag, she slipped toward her seat, her eyes shielded behind her notebook. Somehow, if she didn't look at them they couldn't see her.

She sat down. A stray pencil scooted out of the notebook and clattered to the floor. A few heads went up from their work, but quickly went down again. The class was frighteningly normal—like those scenes in horror movies. The family is sitting there eating or watching TV and you want to yell: Don't put that kid to bed! Don't go down to the basement! Don't step out on the porch! They always do.

She snuck a glance at Mr. Clayton. He was just sitting there talking to Warren Biggs about something on his paper. He looked perfectly normal, not even married.

96

He didn't know. She should have realized that he wouldn't know yet. Why would he go look at his car in the middle of the school day? He hardly even went out at recess time the way he was supposed to. So she had a little more time. For the life of her she didn't know whether to be relieved or sorry. All at once she knew—knew that all she wanted was for it to be over and done. She wasn't sure she could stand waiting any longer.

He had finished talking to Warren. Now he was coming her way. Her hands were freezing and sweaty at the same time. Her mouth felt full of cotton.

"Vinnie." His voice was normal.

"Vinnie," he said again from just above her, "are you all right?"

She nodded, still not daring to speak or even to look at him. She handed him Grandma's note.

"We're catching up on our journal entries about our vacation reading."

She nodded again and eased her journal out from under her seat—carefully, so it wouldn't knock anything else to the floor.

"Okay?" he asked.

"Yessir," she managed to squeak.

Work helped. It took her a while to remember anything about the book she had been reading—a hundred years ago in another lifetime. There was a dog in it. She remembered that much. And a boy who had lied to keep the dog. He had to lie. If he didn't the dog's owner might kill it. The story came back in a rush. She wrote furiously. When her pencil point broke, she didn't sharpen it. She got out another pencil, a stubby one with a dull point, and scratched on as though by covering the white pages everything would be hidden.

"Mr. Clayton." The AP's voice was softer than usual.

but at the sound of it, every head went up and turned toward the door. The man had a peculiar expression on his face, "like the cat that swallowed the ostrich," Grandma would have said. Vinnie felt a strange need to giggle. So this is how it would happen.

Mr. Clayton bolted from his desk and was out in the hall with the door shut behind him before anyone had a chance to breathe twice.

Gary tiptoed to the door and put his ear against the crack. The others were leaning halfway out of their seats—Vinnie, too, when she saw it was the thing to do, but a little later than the rest.

"What are they saying?" "What's going on?" they whispered.

Gary put his finger to his mouth to shut them up and cupped his hand around his ear. To their horror the door began to open. Gary leaped to his seat like a Superman film run backward.

Mr. Clayton put his face in the door. This was it. His face was as gray as a sidewalk. Vinnie's head drooped. It was so heavy, she felt it might break off her neck if she tried to lift it. She waited to hear her name.

"Lupe," he was saying. "May I see you in the hall for a moment, please?"

Lupe? Why would they want Lupe? She saw me do it. She's the witness. She tattled on me. She's always popping up in strange places at funny times. She must have seen me do it and told the AP I did it. Not that anyone would need to tell. I put my stupid initials there myself—

No. A wave of something like relief swept over her. Her head felt light. I put my *real* initials—LM—Lavinia Matthews. The AP thinks Lupe—Lupe Mahoney—did it. And why not? She's the graffiti queen. She would be the first person the AP would suspect. He hates her.

Lupe got up from her seat and headed toward the door. She didn't look at all worried.

"I guess you'd better collect your things," Mr. Clayton said in a sad, tired voice.

Lupe turned and went to the cloakroom. She emerged carrying her worn, old lady's full-length coat and her oversized woman's purse that she used for a book bag. Then she went to her desk, and with every eye in the class upon her, stooped in the aisle to get her things from under the seat. Her long skirt fanned about her on the floor. Her hair hid her face as she bent to the task of clearing out everything from under the chair.

At last she shook back her hair and stood up. Her face was still, without any expression that Vinnie could read.

She strode across the rear of the classroom like a queen of olden days going to have her head chopped off. They all watched with horrified fascination. She held her head high, not looking at anyone. As she turned to go toward the door, she came past Vinnie and her hand brushed the edge of Vinnie's desktop. And then she was gone. Vinnie looked at the place Lupe had touched.

There sat a little plastic bow. The metal prong was open and on its tip something was flaking off. Red. Like dried blood.

Vinnie clamped her fist on it, looking around, her heart pounding. But she needn't have worried. No one was watching her. They were all watching Mr. Clayton as he gently put his arm on Lupe's shoulder and guided her out into the hall, where the AP was waiting.

12

*S*he lifted her hips slightly so she could shove the barrette deep into the pocket of her jeans. It was a miracle that she had worn them. Only one of her school dresses had any pockets and they were useless little shallow patches just for show—nothing would be safe in them.

The metal prong was poking into her thigh. It hurt, but somehow it was meant to. Why had Lupe just put it on her desk and walked out? Why hadn't she saved it to show to someone?

Lupe knew. She had to know who had scratched Mr. Clayton's car. She was probably down there in the office this minute telling them. But why didn't she keep the proof? Mr. Clayton would have recognized at once whose barrette it was. No one else in the class wore them. The other girls probably thought they were babyish. They *were* babyish. Mr. Clayton should have known that. It was his fault. He should never have given the silly, baby things to her.

Any minute now the door would open, and they would come and get her. The class buzzed quietly like visitors in a funeral parlor. She remembered that. She had made them take her to the funeral home. Home. What a dumb word for a place where all you did was go say good-bye to dead people.

She had been determined to see Daddy, and when Grandma told her she couldn't go, she screamed like a two-year-old in a supermarket until Momma said, "Okay, maybe it's for the best."

When she got to the door, she suddenly changed her mind. It was the smell—sickly sweet of disinfectant and too many flowers. Through the glass she could see the long, gray coffin and hear the solemn buzz of people hovering around. A huge form swooped down and kissed her, like a hawk snatching up a baby rabbit. She grabbed for Momma in terror, but another figure had torn her away.

She was caught in a forest of tall bodies pressing against her, whispering over her head. She couldn't even see Daddy. She needed air. She was going to suffocate. She poked out her elbow to make room. A large, bald-headed face loomed over her, the big mouth opened wide to complain, but then quickly shut as though hinged. Behind her she heard a voice cluck, "Poor child."

And then she pushed really hard. People parted and left an open path for her that led straight to the long, gray box banked with flowers so stiff they didn't look real, so smelly she felt faint. There was a little upholstered stool in front of the coffin. She didn't know then it was for people to kneel on. She thought it had been put there for her to climb up to see. But before she could take a breath, much less climb on it, a man she didn't know snatched her high in the air and held her dangling over the coffin. Her eyes were squeezed shut and she wanted to scream, but she didn't. She forced open her eyes and looked down.

There was a sort of store mannequin lying below her, dressed in Daddy's best suit—the blue one he had bought just before he got sick. Its hands were like wax and its fingernails spookily clean.

The face was all puffy—not really like Daddy's thin face, drawn tight with pain, but sort of smug and uncaring, as though it were sneering at all the fuss. Its fake, thin brown hair was slicked down with a funny straight part. The eyes were shut, the lashes long like Mason's, but otherwise there was nothing in that box that could be Daddy. They'd taken Daddy away and put this wax dummy that was supposed to look like Daddy in his place.

She wriggled so against the man's big hands that he put her down on the floor. When she turned away from the coffin she saw Momma watching her. But by now she was perfectly calm. She had seen a dead person and she hadn't screamed. She hadn't even been really scared. She walked over to Momma and took her hand. They stood there like that, side by side, for what seemed like hours while people came up and said dumb things like how good Daddy looked and what a blessing he wasn't suffering anymore.

After a while Mason appeared. She guessed Sheila from upstairs had brought him because Mason was holding Sheila's hand and chewing gum. Sheila always gave Mason and Vinnie gum, even though Momma didn't really approve. By then most of the crowd had left, and Grandma and Momma, with Vinnie still clinging to her hand, were in the corner talking to the funeral director. Sheila went over to speak to them.

"Vinnie," Momma said, "watch Mason for me, will you?" She didn't want to let go of Momma's hand, but

Momma let go of Vinnie. "Just for a minute, all right? We need to get some business settled . . ."

So she let go of Momma's hand and went over to where Mason was standing, looking small and lost against all the sprays of stern-looking flowers.

"Where's Daddy?" Mason asked her. Sheila had told him that Daddy was here and Mason wanted to see him, so Vinnie took Mason over to the wax man they said was Daddy.

"Get up, Daddy," Mason whispered, tugging at Daddy's sleeve. "Get up."

She was so scared. She didn't want the wax man to get up. After that she told Mason that Daddy was dead. She was mad at Mason for scaring her, and Daddy for dying, and Momma for letting go of her hand. So she told Mason that he was stupid—that no matter what he said he couldn't change Daddy being dead. And she was right. But Mason had never said anything since.

She stuck her hand into her pocket and pushed her finger hard against the barrette prong. It hurt. It was probably bleeding. Carefully, she pulled her hand out. There was a little dent in the pad of her index finger, but already the flesh was plumping up around the tiny chips of red paint. She rubbed her finger against the bottom of her desk. She was sweating again.

The door was opening. Vinnie stared at it, her eyes and mouth dry as chalk. Mr. Clayton came in and closed the door carefully behind him.

His face was drawn and grim and maybe, maybe sad. He was walking hunched over and he sort of slumped into his seat.

The room was perfectly still—silent as a tomb. Where had she heard that? Finally, there was a funny little sound, as though all the class sniffed in a breath at once, and then they were all bent over their desktops, scratching away on their journals.

How could one day stretch out as long as a whole lifetime? She couldn't hurry it in any way. She couldn't speak to anyone. She felt that she was wriggling and squiggling in the air, that a giant had stabbed her with a great steel fork and was lifting her to his mouth. When would he bite? When would her terrifying life come crashing to its sure and horrible end?

Lunch—not the giant's, but her own eerily normal lunch period—came and went. She sat in a corner of the cafeteria by herself. The noises about her seemed cut off, as though she were sitting in an almost soundproof glass cage—a coffin.

Once, later on in the afternoon, Mr. Clayton stopped by her desk. "How're you doing?" he asked. "Feeling any better?"

She couldn't understand at first what he was talking about. Oh—Grandma's note. She nodded but didn't dare look up. She couldn't look him in the face. He would be able to see right inside her. He was sure to know everything then.

By the time the final bell sounded, her whole body was numb—not as though just a foot or a hand was asleep but as if all the circulation to her entire self had been cut off.

Somehow she stumbled to her feet and out the door. She was down the steps and halfway to the street before she remembered Mason. Momma was going to drop him off at school after the appointment in Charlottesville.

Her body was so heavy that she felt like an elephant trying to turn around. Mason was waiting for her, standing beside Mrs. Paxton at the kindergarten-room door.

"There she is," Mrs. Paxton said, her voice a mixture of fake cheer and true relief. "I knew she wouldn't forget you. See? All that worrying for nothing!"

How did Mrs. Paxton figure out that Mason was worried? Vinnie looked at his face. He *did* look worried. When she took his hand, he didn't shake loose.

Usually she tried to talk to or yell at Mason on the way home, depending on how he was behaving. Today she was as mute as he. Now she knew deep in her guts what her head had been telling her for a long time. It was all her fault that Mason didn't talk. She'd done it that night in the funeral home—not on purpose but just by being hateful.

But today was different. Today she'd meant to be hateful. She could still feel the wild, fierce satisfaction of scratching, screeching, the barrette pinched so tight that it cut into her fingers.

And I made them blame Lupe.

A shudder went through her. Even Mason felt it. He looked up, a question in his big, tired eyes, under their long, roofed lashes. Like Daddy's.

She squeezed his fingers in her own. She could feel him trying to pull away as though she were hurting him, but she wouldn't—couldn't—let go until they reached the packed earth of their own front yard. He dashed ahead of her into the house.

Vinnie went straight to her room, dropping her book bag in the middle of the hall. From the door she could see herself almost full length in the mirror over the bureau, long, stringy hair falling across her narrow face. Suddenly, she knew what she had to do. She went into her mother's room, tearing through the dresser drawers until she found the sewing scissors. Then, without looking in the mirror, she began to whack off all her hair.

Someone was watching her. She turned. Mason was standing in the doorway. He had Agnes dangling under his left arm. His right thumb was in his mouth.

"Get out."

He didn't move.

"You heard me. Get out."

His eyes went to the scissors and he blinked, but he didn't move.

"Get out! Get out! Get out!" she screamed, dropping the scissors. "And give me Agnes!" She grabbed the rag doll's legs and snatched her away. "I don't ever want to see your stupid face again as long as I live." He blinked rapidly, his long, beautiful lashes sweeping his cheek each time.

Vinnie swung the doll and whapped Mason across the face. His thin, little hand flew to his cheek, and, still covering the place where she had struck him, he turned and ran.

She slammed the door after him and turned to the mirror. What had she done? She threw Agnes on Momma's bed and picked up the scissors again. What had she done? She cut off a long piece of hair that was sticking straight out. Then she saw that the other side was too long. She hacked at it. Then back to the first side, which—

It was no use. She couldn't do anything right. She flung herself on Momma's bed, hugging Agnes to her as though she, not Mason, were the five-year-old, and cried and cried and cried.

13

"*L*avinia? Have you seen Mason?"

Vinnie woke with a start. She was lying on Momma's bed, her nose smushed into a damp spot on the spread. She sat up.

"What *have* you done to your hair?"

Vinnie's hand went up. She felt a spike of hair sticking out above her ear.

"I cut it," she said. Her face felt tight and dried up from too much crying.

"Have you seen Mason?" her grandmother asked again, obviously more worried about Mason than about Vinnie or her hair.

"I walked him home."

"Yes, I know. But that was an hour ago. He doesn't seem to be anywhere around. I hoped he was in here with you—that you were playing hide-and-seek or—or something," she said lamely.

I told him, Vinnie remembered, I told him I never wanted to see him again. "He's got to be somewhere!"

"I've looked everywhere I can think of—the closets, the packing boxes in the basement, even the laundry basket." Grandma almost smiled. "I've called and called. I know he likes to play tricks on us, but I've never known him to just up and disappear."

I told him to go away—that I never wanted to see him again as long as I lived. If he could stop talking, he might disappear as well.

"Do you have any ideas? I *hate* to call Grace. She'll be frantic, and I'm sure he's right here under our noses."

But he wasn't. They even put the stepladder up so they could reach the trapdoor to the attic and look up there. Vinnie opened the dryer and the washer and went once more through every box in the basement and every closet. They lay down on their stomachs and looked under all the beds, even under the living room couch, which was too low for a skinny cat to slide under, much less a five-year-old boy.

I told him to go away. "He's not in the house."

"Then where on earth?"

"I don't know. I'll find him though."

"No. I don't want you going out. It'll be dark before long and I can't have the two of you—" Grandma started for the kitchen. "I'm calling your mother. It'll be better if we have the car. You wait right there. Don't you go off anywhere, you hear me?"

As soon as Grandma got on the phone, Vinnie left. She had no idea where to start looking. Where would Mason go? She tried to think like Mason, but her head turned to stone. She couldn't imagine. Where would he go? Not to school. He didn't like school. He didn't like anyplace where Momma wasn't. They didn't go many places. They went to the grocery store. They went to the convenience store. They'd gone a couple of times to Grandma's church, but Mason was so wild and jumpy in his Sunday school class that Momma decided to wait until he got better before she took him back.

The convenience store. Mason liked the convenience store. It had gum and candy and all the things Momma didn't like him to have. Why he should go there, she didn't know. It wasn't as if he had any money to spend. But she had to look somewhere. It was cold and almost dusk. He'd probably find a place where he could get warm.

He wasn't there. She walked around all the short aisles several times to be sure. She looked in the ladies' room, and when she thought the woman at the counter was busy, she opened the men's room door as well.

"Hey, girlie!" A man in a convenience store jacket was standing over her.

"I—I lost my little brother," she managed to stammer out.

"Well, he ain't in there."

"No sir." She felt like a fool but desperation made her ask, "I don't guess you've seen him? He's got light brown hair and he's about this high."

"There was a little kid in here a while ago, Leroy," the woman clerk yelled over. "Maybe an hour ago? I thought he was with that Mahoney girl. I was kind of watching them both, you know."

Lupe. Mason liked Lupe. "Did he leave with her?"

"I dunno. Least when she left, I realized he was gone, too."

Vinnie raced out, without even thanking them. She began to run but, in the cold, she was soon out of breath. It was all right, though; if he was with Lupe, he was safe.

Her ears were freezing, but Vinnie walked fast enough to raise a sweat under her jacket. At first she followed along the side of the tracks, afraid that a train might catch her, though in the three months she'd lived in Brownsville, she'd never seen or heard a train. Indeed, the tracks were overgrown with weeds, now brittle with frost.

She knew it was a long way—it had seemed so when they went to buy the pumpkin—but cold as she was and despite the rough path, she was fiercely determined to be the one to find Mason and bring him safely home. As she walked through the edge of town, she feared that some nosy grown-up might see her from one of the houses and come out and question her. No one did, and she soon left the last house behind.

She turned up the collar of her jacket against the wind. Her chopped hair scratched her neck. She jumped over the rail to walk between the tracks. Despite the weeds, the ties and gravel made something of a path, and she could walk much faster there than in the tangled growth along the side.

Behind the rusting skeleton of the railroad trestle, the sun was sinking fast into the faraway hills. At first Vinnie didn't recognize the pumpkin patch. Frost had blackened the green jungle of October into a shriveled mass. She could see a blob of orange here and there. Vinnie left the tracks, making her way down a weedy slope to the country road. The old door still sat there on the sawhorses in the brown grass next to the pavement, though the sign had fallen off and rain had washed away the chalked words.

She half slid, half stumbled down the path toward the blackened field. In the floor of the bowl, the stumps of frost-killed vines scraped against her jeans, but she kept pushing her way forward, straight for the dim light in the shack window. "Let him be there," she prayed. "Let him be safe."

Until she stepped up on the stoop, Vinnie hadn't thought what Lupe might say or do. She'd only thought that she must find Mason. Now she felt a baseball rising in her throat as she raised her hand to the door. She couldn't let anything stop her. She had to find Mason. Vinnie swallowed hard and knocked.

Lupe opened the door a crack. "You cut your hair," she said. "Yourself."

"Mason." It was all she could manage.

"Your brother?"

"Isn't he here?" She pushed past Lupe into the house. An old woman was standing at a black iron stove, stirring something in a pot. She turned to gape at Vinnie, her open mouth showing a tooth missing. "Mason!" Vinnie cried into the room, ignoring the woman. "It's me, Vinnie."

"Mason?" the woman asked Lupe, puzzled. "Who's this Mason?"

"He isn't here, Vinnie," Lupe said. "How come you think he's here?"

"He left with you. From the convenience store. They told me."

"I was in there a while ago, but I never saw your brother," she said. "If I'd seen him I would have brought him straight home."

She wasn't lying. Vinnie knew she wasn't. She turned to go.

"Wait. I'll get my coat."

Lupe caught up with Vinnie in the patch. "You got any idea where we ought to look?"

Vinnie shook her head. "I told him to go away," she

111

said, trying to keep back the tears. "I told him I never wanted to see him again."

"Oh my God." Lupe's head was up, alert.

"What?"

"Shh. Listen."

At first Vinnie thought it was just the distant cry of some little animal lost out there in the near darkness. Then she heard it again.

"Da-dee!"

She opened her mouth to scream, but Lupe clamped a hand over her face. "Turn around carefully, now," she whispered, "but don't, whatever you do, don't yell. I think I see him." She put her hand on Vinnie's shoulder. "Up there."

Vinnie gasped. High above them on the trestle there was a small dark blot against the dying sky.

"You walk over close so you can talk to him. But no yelling, you hear? Just natural and easy. Like the cops in the movies. I'll go up and around and get him, okay?"

Vinnie nodded. She made her way through the black vines until she was a few yards from the foot of the trestle. Then she looked up. She couldn't see his face. But his little head, his whole little bent-over body was shaking. He seemed to be clutching the rail with both hands. Don't, please God, don't let him fall.

"Mason," she said softly, "it's me, Vinnie. Don't look down at me, okay? Just wait quietly. It's going to be all right." What should she say? What could she do? "Just hold on a little while longer, okay?" She remembered the song Daddy used to sing to make the time go by:

"'This old man,'" she sang just loud enough so that he could hear,

"This old man, he played one,
He played knick knack on my thumb.

With a knick knack paddy wack,
Give your dog a bone,
This old man came rolling home."

As she sang it, verse after verse—softly so he wouldn't hear the fright in her voice—she could see, out of the corner of her eye, a dark, lean figure leaping up the side of the hill, surefooted as a mountain cat. At last she reached the rim of the giant bowl in which Vinnie stood, disappearing briefly and reappearing in a crouch, inching on all fours out across the trestle toward the place where Mason clung.

"'This old man, he played nine . . .'" Lupe had reached him. Vinnie stopped singing. Above her, on the track, she could hear, not the words, but a gentle urging. Her heart stopped as she saw Mason suddenly let go of whatever he was clutching and grab Lupe's neck. She watched them crawl back, Mason clinging under Lupe, his arms and legs wrapped around her like a monkey child holding onto its mother. It wasn't until they were off the trestle that Lupe stood up. For a moment, they were out of sight and then she could see their dark shapes up on the road, starting down the slope, Lupe still carrying Mason on her chest.

Vinnie began to yell. She ran, as well as she could across the withered vines, running and yelling and tripping and catching herself. They met at the edge of the patch.

"Mason," she screamed. "You scared me to death! You could have killed yourself." She flung her arms around both of them and began to cry. "Why did you go up there, you stu— Oh, Mason, what would I do if something happened to you?"

"I dunno."

Except for that little strangled cry, she hadn't heard his

voice for more than three months, so when he spoke, she looked to see if it might have been Lupe.

But Lupe was telling her to get out of the way. "He's near to frozen," she was saying. "We got to get him warm." Vinnie didn't move. "In the house!"

The three of them went into the shack. Lupe's grandmother was sitting in a chair by the iron stove. She was wearing the same kind of ankle-length dress that Lupe wore, but she was stouter and her long hair was gray. She smiled shyly and half made as if to rise when they came in. Lupe sat Mason down on the only bed in the room, grabbing up the bedclothes to swaddle around him. "Help me wrap him up," she commanded.

Vinnie obeyed. Mason blinked at her. Had she just imagined his voice in the pumpkin patch? She put her arms around him and held him tight to her. He was shivering against the quilt.

"Here," said Lupe and shoved a cup toward him.

He looked in. "I'm not allowed coffee," he said.

"You are in my house," Lupe said. "Drink."

He took a sip, making a face. He held it out to Lupe. "I want more sugar," he said.

"Say 'please,'" Lupe said.

"Please," he said.

It was like some kind of tea party out of *Alice in Wonderland*. They were all four of them drinking Lupe's terrible black coffee loaded with sugar, the sweet unable to mask the bitterness. The old lady, nodding and smiling in her chair, occasionally got up to stir the steaming pot on the stove. Vinnie huddled close to Mason on the bed, their feet swinging against the bedclothes, their legs too short to touch the floor. Lupe shuffled around among them, her huge black sneakers squeaking on the worn linoleum.

"You want to stay and have some stew with me and the girl?" the old lady asked.

"We'd better go," Vinnie said. "It's dark and they'll be worried sick about Mason."

"I'll help you carry him," Lupe said. "He's had some kinda day."

As they walked, Lupe carrying Mason in the quilt she'd wrapped around him earlier, Vinnie tried to think what to say. But nothing was good enough. When at last they were at Grandma's front door, and Lupe had put Mason on his feet and begun to fold the quilt, Vinnie said: "Tomorrow—tomorrow I'll tell Mr. Clayton about—you know."

Lupe looked up. "You don't need to on my account."

"Yeah," Vinnie said. "Yeah, I do."

"Okay," Lupe said. "But do something for me first, all right?"

"Sure," Vinnie said. Her heart skipped a beat, but after all that had happened, she had to promise.

"Get your mother or your grandmother or somebody to fix your hair."

14

As soon as Vinnie opened the door, Grandma yelled something into the kitchen phone and came racing down the hall. She threw her arms around both of them at once, sobbing and thanking the dear Lord.

After a bit, Mason pulled away, and Vinnie was left with Grandma as the woman cried and stroked her bristly hair. "You shouldn't have gone out. I told you not to. We were crazy with worry."

"It's okay, Grandma." She touched Grandma's brown, speckled arm. "It's okay." She looked around. "Where's Momma?" She wanted to be the one to tell Momma about Mason.

"Your momma's on the way. I was on the phone with her when you walked in. Oh, thank you, Lord." And then in the same breath, "You kids want some soda or something?"

They were sitting at the kitchen table drinking flat diet cola when Momma threw open the front door and came running down the hall. Vinnie jumped up and ran to meet her. Momma fell on her knees as she grabbed Vinnie to her. "Oh, my babies." She was crying as though a dam had broken inside her.

"Oh, Momma," Vinnie was crying, too. "I'm so sorry. I'm so sorry."

Momma hugged her so tightly that Vinnie's whole body shook with Momma's sobs.

"Momma?" Mason had slid off the kitchen chair and come to where they were huddled together on the hall floor. He reached over to pat Momma's heaving back. "Don't cry, Momma," he said. "Please don't cry."

Momma raised her head off Vinnie's shoulder. "Mason?"

"He can talk, Momma. Can't you, Mason?" For a moment she was afraid. Grandma had come from the kitchen and everyone was staring at him. It seemed forever before Mason nodded.

"Yeah," he said.

She tried to write a poem about everything that had happened, but she had to give up. It was too hard to put it all together on one page. The poem was going to be about Lupe, the flip-flop girl, whose real name was Maria Guadalupé after some Spanish saint, and whose Irish father was sent to prison for a crime Vinnie was sure he did not do. As she was writing she thought of her own father, who had suffered and died and he hadn't done anything wrong either. Then, while she was trying to work that out, she remembered how Lupe was always getting in trouble for nothing. And Vinnie herself—a flip-flop girl of the worst kind. Yet Lupe had helped her, had saved both her and Mason. Could a single poem include all that, with Momma and Grandma and all their troubles in there, too? Plus Mr. Clayton?

She told Mr. Clayton, as she promised. She went early to school to get it over with. She could hardly get the words out. Somehow it was all mixed up with Daddy dying and Mason and, of course, Lupe. She had hurt them all. Mr. Clayton, too.

He was quiet for a long time, letting her cry without interrupting. "Thanks, Vinnie," he said finally. "I just couldn't believe Lupe had done it." He ran his big hand through his hair and hurried on. "I couldn't have believed you did it either, but . . . well . . . after all, it's just a car, isn't it? Not a person—not a living creature."

She wiped her nose with the tissue he'd handed her and searched his face. He really meant it. "I'll pay," she said.

"The insurance—" he began and then stopped. "If you want to help with the deductible—that's fifty dollars."

So, she wouldn't have much time for poetry. She told Lupe about the deductible, and once more Lupe came to her rescue. She got Mrs. Winston to hire Vinnie, too. After walking Mason home, Vinnie raced back to the big white house where she and Lupe cleaned and ran errands and did odd jobs for Mrs. Winston. The old lady was pretty tight with her money. Vinnie wouldn't earn fifty dollars in her whole lifetime probably, but she'd get together what she could to pay back Mr. Clayton.

She wasn't sure how Mr. Clayton managed it. The day Vinnie talked to him, he drove out to Lupe's house and brought her back to school. He took her straight to the office, where the principal and Mr. Sharp sort of apologized for suspending her. Mr. Clayton said afterward that there was no reason to bring up Vinnie's name. The "incident" had occurred off school property, after all.

Mason didn't fit into poetry. The doctor in Charlottesville was delighted. He even hinted that he'd been a big help to Mason, that, thanks to him, Mason was going to be all right. Momma didn't bother to argue. Mason was talking and eating. That was what mattered. He still misbehaved sometimes, but it was a kind of normal—swatting other kids on the playground, cutting up in class—noisy misbehaving, so Mrs. Paxton could relax and act like a grown-up about it. Mason still liked to suck his thumb. But Momma said he would probably outgrow thumb-sucking before he went off to college.

Now that he was talking, Mason and Vinnie sometimes talked in bed after the lights were out and they were supposed to be going to sleep. She told him about Daddy. He remembered about Daddy making funny faces at him, but he couldn't remember half the things about Daddy that Vinnie could. She wanted him to know what a great daddy they'd had. Besides, if she kept telling him, it would keep her from forgetting.

"Knock knock," she said.

"What?"

"You're supposed to say 'Who's there?'"

"Why?"

"Because that's how you do knock-knock jokes, Mason."

"Okay. Who's there?"

"Mason."

"Mason? I'm Mason."

"I know, stupid. But you're supposed to say 'Mason who?'"

"Why?"

"So we can do the joke."

"Oh. Okay. Mason who?"

"May sun shine on you."

He laughed like crazy in the dark. The room was quiet

ABOUT THE AUTHOR

KATHERINE PATERSON'S books have received wide acclaim and been published in twenty languages. Among her many literary honors are two Newbery Medals, for *Bridge to Terabithia* and *Jacob Have I Loved,* and two National Book Awards. Her most recent novel, *Lyddie,* has been chosen as the U.S. representative for Writing on the biennial Honor List of the International Board on Books for Young People (IBBY).

The parents of four children, Mrs. Paterson and her husband live in Barre, Vermont.